Rosemary Beach Kisses

Rosemary Beach Kisses

Kisses

Love Along Hwy 30A
Book Six

Melissa Chambers

Copyright 2021 Melissa Chambers. All rights reserved.
First Edition October 2021

Perry Evans Press

ISBN: 978-1-7324156-9-0

Edited by The Proof Is in the Reading
Cover image from iStock

melissachambers.com

Also by Melissa Chambers

Love Along Hwy 30A Series:

Seaside Sweets

Seacrest Sunsets

Seagrove Secrets

WaterColor Wishes

Grayton Beach Dreams

Destiny Dunes Series:

Down for Her

Up for Seconds

Coming Around

In His Heart

Over the Moon

Young Adult titles:

The Summer Before Forever (Before Forever #1)

Falling for Forever (Before Forever #2)

Courting Carlyn (Standalone)

For J.

Chapter One

Please just think about it. Money is no object, and I'll make it worth your while.

Meade Forbes's conversations with the billionaire had gotten oddly comfortable. Though one of the richest people on earth, he certainly wasn't above begging. And what was he doing texting her directly anyway? He had people for that.

He wanted her, and he wasn't afraid to let her know how much. If this was a guy she'd met at a bar, she'd consider it stalking by the number of times he'd reached out to her. But he wasn't after Meade for a fling. He wanted her full-time. The question was…did she want him?

She tossed her phone into her purse and got out of her car, heading toward the library. As she approached the circulation desk, her heartbeat accelerated as she blinked the Clark Kent cutie into focus. It was the guy she had met at her friend

Desiree's art showing at that fancy house in Alys Beach back in July.

He'd mentioned having seen her at the library...even knew the last book she had read. At the time, she couldn't decide if that was cute or creepy. Then after he'd walked away, leaving her wishing he wouldn't have, she decided she didn't mind the intrusion.

Every time she'd come into the library since then, she'd glanced around for him. She'd always come up empty, but here she was, six weeks later, and there he stood. He'd been dressed up at the party, but now he wore a T-shirt and jeans, and his body wasn't hidden like it had been in his dress pants and button-down. The muscles in his biceps filled out the T-shirt sleeves quite nicely. He picked up a stack of books and walked through a doorway, leaving the circulation desk and giving her a view of his very grabbable ass.

The teenage girl who was sometimes working when she came in walked up to the counter. "Whatcha got there?"

"I'm returning these books, but there's a page missing in this one. I wanted to point it out to you."

"Jerk. What kind of psychopath rips a page out of a library book?" she asked Meade.

"Not cool, right?"

"I'll get these checked in," the girl said, taking the stack. She looked at Meade's T-shirt. "I'm sorry, but you have the most perfect collection of female rock star T-shirts ever."

Meade looked down at her shirt, trying to remember which one she put on. "Oh. Thank you."

"I had no idea who Blondie was, but after seeing your T-shirt last time, I totally added her to my playlist, and she is like freaking awesome."

Meade refrained from explaining that Blondie was a band and Debbie Harry was the lead singer. "Yeah, pretty awesome."

"Who is Liz Phair?" The girl had her phone out with her thumbs flying across the screen.

"Look up 'Supernova,'" Meade said.

The girl shoved an earbud in one ear and stood there, bobbing her head. "Stellar."

Meade hated to bug her, but she did need her for one more thing. "Umm, I had a hold on a book that's come in."

"What's your last name again?" she asked.

"Bottoms," Meade said, giving the name of the woman who she rented her efficiency apartment from. Meade had mentioned her love for the library and how she couldn't get a card since she was a short-term renter, and the woman had sent Meade her local library card in the mail. Meade was consistent with her rent and didn't complain about anything, which paid off.

The girl walked over to a shelf behind her, and the nerd came back through the doorway. When he saw Meade, he stopped in his tracks and pointed. "Meade, right?"

Meade didn't like the way her stomach fluttered when he remembered her name. Hot as this guy was turning out to be, she was not into nerds. Meade went for younger guys with no interest in discussing protons, neutrons, or whether or not black holes were real or theoretical. Meade liked men who had no idea who Neil deGrasse Tyson was, even though he'd been the reason she'd become interested in astrophysics.

Meade shifted her weight backward, moving a few inches away.

The guy put both hands on his chest. "I'm Ryder, Desiree's friend. We met this past summer."

Meade looked down, nodding. "I remember."

The young girl came back over, and he glanced at the book in her hand. "Mae Jemison." He thought about it a moment with his eyes shut, and then opened them. "Astronaut, right?"

The girl rolled her eyes. "What was your first clue?" She showed the book cover to Meade, which contained the word astronaut.

"I didn't see that, I swear," he said.

Meade just glanced at him and then dug in her purse for her library card, unsure what to make of him.

"Don't you have books to shelve?" the girl asked him.

He held up both hands like he was being robbed and backed away. "I'm going." He gave Meade a smile before making his exit.

The girl let out an exhaustive sigh, taking Meade's library card from her. "Could he be more obvious?"

Meade didn't say anything, not sure what she meant.

"Cree-pee," the girl said in a sing-song, watching the guy push a cart down an aisle. "I mean, you're just trying to come in here and read a library book. You shouldn't be accosted by some weird dude."

"I know, right?" Meade said conspiratorially, not wanting to be left out of the teenage bonding.

She waved Meade off. "He's harmless. It's not like he's going to look up your address in this computer and go over to your house and watch you sleep at night."

Meade paused, looking at this girl, rethinking having used the library card.

She slid the book to Meade. "He hasn't dated anyone in like a million years. I don't think the geek would have a clue how to even ask."

Meade narrowed her gaze at the girl. "You've known him a while?"

"Oh yeah. He's my dad."

Meade was not expecting that.

"We've got a new couch back in autobiographies." The girl grabbed Meade's returned books. "You should check it out." She headed off.

A dad. Figured. Meade did not want to get mixed up with a guy who came with a sassy teenage daughter who Meade very much liked, but who was probably not a picnic twenty-four seven. She should take this book and head to her favorite spot on the beach. But she did want to check out that new couch. And she wasn't quite ready to leave just yet. Nothing made her happier than a library.

The girl at the front desk had not been lying about the couch. It was super comfortable. Meade could've taken a nap on it if the book hadn't held her attention. She was ready to go home though and get something to eat. She hadn't eaten since a midmorning bagel. She had to get better about eating, but not today. Her weight was always up and down. She didn't mind going hungry all day, but then when she did eat, it wasn't anything healthy. For that reason, she carried too much weight in her stomach...just the right amount in her boobs and butt though. If she could lop off her belly, she'd be thrilled.

She stood up and stretched, ready to take the book to the return bin. On her way there, she spotted the girl from the front desk sitting at a table with a desk lamp, frowning as she used her pencil eraser and she pinched her forehead.

She approached the girl. "What are you working on?"

She met Meade's gaze and her shoulders fell. "Freaking calc. It's kicking my ass."

Meade rewound her brain back to high school. It's not like Meade had thought about calculus recently, but her brain never let go of anything, unfortunately.

"Do you need some help?"

The girl met her with a hopeful gaze. "Do you know calc?"

"May I see your book?"

Her hopeful expression dropped, and she handed Meade the book. "My dad tells me to watch a video. I think he just doesn't know how to help me. I've been great in math my whole life, which is why I'm in calc as a sophomore, but the semester just started, and I'm already behind."

Meade settled into the chair next to her, flipping to the start of the section. "Give me a minute with this. Take a walk or something. Listen to that Liz Phair song," she said with a smile.

"Really?"

"Go," Meade said, already settling in with the book.

By the time the girl got back, Meade had worked a few problems. The girl sat down, staring at the paper in front of Meade with wild eyes. "Did you just do that?"

"The way they are teaching this is messed up, but I assume that's how your teacher wants it done."

The girl shuffled into her seat, looking at the paper in amazement.

"What's your name?" Meade asked.

"Annabella."

"I'm Meade."

"Wait," she said, squinting at Meade. "I thought your name was Emily."

"Emily is the woman whose house I'm renting. She's letting me use her library card."

She waggled her eyebrows. "Rebel. Just like me."

Meade handed her the pencil. "Let's do some calc, rebel."

Ryder had never considered himself a stalker, but no doubt he had been stalking his daughter with the very attractive Meade for the past hour. He found them sitting together and was ready to pounce on Annabella for not doing her homework when he overheard number talk. Meade had to be a math teacher the way she was explaining the concepts to Annabella with such assuredness and authority, but in a way that was digestible. Ryder did not have that kind of patience. When he tried to help his daughter with math, he found the new way they taught it tripped him up. He referred her to videos recorded in the past few years so she was learning the right way. But Meade understood the new way.

The book was closed now, and the two of them were exchanging phone numbers. Was that appropriate to do with a teacher?

He came out from his hiding place and made a production of walking over so he didn't seem stealthy. "Did the two of you solve the world's equations?"

"Dad, Meade is fantastic. She just taught me everything I needed for the test. I'm going to ace it."

"That's great, but I don't think you should be calling her Meade. What's your last name?" he said to the beautiful blonde.

She waved him off. "Just Meade."

"Are you a teacher at the school?"

Meade cracked up. "Hell, no."

"Meade works as a bartender on the beach," Annabella said. "Is that not the coolest ever?"

Ryder was confused. This highly intelligent woman wasn't a teacher or a professor? Or didn't have some top-level corporate job?

Meade stood, shouldering her purse. "Text me and let me know how the test goes."

"For sure," Annabella said, and then her phone dinged, and she was laser-focused on it as she thumbed away.

Meade walked toward the door, and Ryder followed after her. "So, you're not a math teacher?"

"God, no. I don't like kids. No offense. Your kid seems cool."

"You don't have kids of your own in school?"

"No." She winced, shaking her shoulders.

"Then how did you know how to do calculus so well?"

She mumbled something that sounded like *I don't know* as she tossed her book in the return. Had she already read it?

"Can I give you some money for the tutoring?"

She gave him a strange look as she pushed open the door. "I'm not gonna take your money."

"What about dinner? Will you take that?"

She stopped on the sidewalk. "Look, it was no big deal."

"It was to Annabella. I should've gotten her a tutor already. I just kept thinking she would catch on eventually. She's always been good in math."

"She's a smart girl. It was a tricky concept."

"Can we take you out to dinner to say thank you?"

"Like, today?"

"Yeah, right now."

She glanced at the parking lot and then back at him. "Annabella's mother wouldn't have a problem with that?"

Ryder looked down at his shoes. "She's not in the picture."

"I'm sorry."

"Me too...for Annabella's sake."

Annabella came out the front door and joined them.

"I was just asking Meade if we could take her out to dinner tonight for helping you with your homework."

"Cool. Where are we going?" Annabella asked.

"Ladies' choice," Ryder said, motioning at Meade.

"Can we go to Tilly's Tavern?" his daughter asked.

He gave her a skeptical look. Tilly's Tavern was more of a bar than a restaurant. "Do they even sell food?"

"Oh totally. Their chicken tenders are really good."

"Chicken tenders? Seriously?" he asked her.

"I love Tilly's Tavern," Meade said, smiling at Annabella. "That's my choice."

Ryder looked between his daughter and this woman he found himself more than intrigued with. He'd thought she was attractive when he'd first seen her at Desiree's art showing in July. She'd been dressed to kill in heels and a dress with a plunging neckline, but standing here in cutoff jeans and a T-shirt with her blond hair tied into a messy little bun on top of her head and wisps hanging out all over, he was even more attracted to her.

They both nodded and smiled at him. He tossed up his hands. "All right, then. Tilly's Tavern."

"I'll meet you there," Meade said, and then she was off, leaving him curious and a little smitten.

Chapter Two

As soon as they got to the restaurant, Annabella was craning her neck, scouring the joint. They had barely ordered their drinks when Annabella lit up. "Oh my gosh. It's Grace Hinton and her group."

Meade leaned in conspiratorially. "Who is Grace Hinton?"

"I've been trying to get in with them for like years."

"We've only been here a little over a year," Ryder said.

Annabella gave him an irritated wave off, and then her eyes went wide. "Oh my God. She's coming over here." She adjusted in her seat.

Grace narrowed her gaze at Meade. "You work at the Tiki bar on Rosemary Beach, don't you?"

"Yep," Meade said.

Grace looked between Annabella and Meade. "This is your mom?"

"No." When the expression on Grace's face dropped, Annabella said, "She's my dad's girlfriend."

Ryder gave his daughter a quizzical look, and then glanced at Meade for a reaction, but she was too busy looking Grace up and down.

"Cool," Grace said. "We're just hanging over there watching the band. You could come if you wanted."

Annabella shrugged. "I might."

Grace walked away, and Annabella grabbed Ryder's forearm. "Dad, please."

"I thought we were having dinner to thank Meade for her help."

"Ryder, come on," Meade said with a look on her face like he was the clueless dad that he was. Even so, he liked hearing his name come off her tongue.

"I assume I should order you the chicken tenders?"

She grinned, giving him a kiss on the cheek. "Thanks, Dad." She jumped up and was off.

"An actual kiss. I haven't gotten one of those since she was ten."

"I have a feeling this Grace Hinton is a bigger deal than you know."

"Do you know this kid? She seemed to know you."

"No, but I've known plenty of her type in my time. She can make or break a high school reputation. Sucks, but it's true."

"Are you speaking from experience?"

Meade rolled her eyes. "You don't wanna know."

"I think I do."

"I wasn't necessarily popular in high school."

"I can't imagine that. A girl as attractive as you are."

She gave him a look.

He held up a hand. "Sorry. I just call them like I see them." The server brought their drinks, and they ordered their food. When she walked away, he said, "I think I can guess what your problem was in high school."

"Oh yeah?"

"You were too smart."

Meade lifted an eyebrow. "Does it take one to know one?"

"I did okay, but I have a feeling you're on a different level of smart than I am."

"What would make you say something like that?"

"Because I see the books you read for fun."

"Stalker."

"Just interested," he said. She gave him a sly look with those intensely blue eyes he was starting to fall into. "How did you know that calculus?"

She shrugged. "I just read the chapter."

"Yeah, but it had to have been, what, fifteen years ago that you were in college?"

"Are you trying to guess my age?"

"Maybe. I think you're probably close to my age."

"What's your age?"

"I'm thirty-eight."

Meade narrowed her gaze at him. "What happened to you, by the way?"

"What do you mean?"

"You haven't been at the library for a while."

This made Ryder smile. "You were looking for

me?"

"No, I wasn't looking for you. You said you worked there when I met you back in July. Then you disappeared."

"Work got hairy. The library's a volunteer job, so they can't really fire me."

She nodded and glanced around.

"You were looking for me, weren't you?" he asked, knowing he was pushing his luck, but he had gone into the friend zone too many times not to have learned his lesson.

She shook her head. "Don't get any ideas. Seriously, I don't date guys like you."

"What's that supposed to mean?"

"It just means you're nothing like the guys I date."

"What are those guys like?"

Meade glanced around, honing in on a server who seemed pleased to get her attention. She put her gaze back on Ryder.

"That guy?" he asked. "He's like twenty."

She shrugged. "I'm not interested in anything long-term. Younger guys usually aren't either."

"What's wrong with long-term?"

Meade messed with her straw. "I'm not sure what I'm doing."

He cocked his head to the side, waiting for her to elaborate, but she didn't. "Do you mean as far as dating goes or…"

"Just in general. I don't like commitments."

"On a personal level or…"

"On any level. I have an overbearing family. They expect big things from me. I like to disappoint them." She looked him in the eye, a challenge.

"And that guy you just indicated… He would be a disappointment for them?"

"Oh yeah. Especially my sister. She would have a coronary."

"Tell me about your sister," he said, surprising himself with how interested he was in this woman and her backstory.

Meade sighed. "Maya is perfect in every way possible. She has a high-powered job. She's in shape and eats clean and healthy every day. She works out and is perfectly toned. She's married to the hottest guy in Panama City, no argument from anyone who has seen him. And he worships her and treats her like a queen. She has approval from my parents on everything she does. And she completely disapproves of me in every way, shape, and form."

"That sounds intense. And maybe a little exaggerated?"

"Unfortunately, I'm not exaggerating. That is my sister."

"Where is your family from? Panama City?"

"No, we're from Indianapolis. Maya came down here on vacation and fell in love with Bo Harrison. Have you ever seen Harrison Pool Supply?"

"In Panama City Beach, right?"

"That's Bo's store."

"I've met him a time or two around Desiree. I talked to him that night at her art showing. He was a really nice guy."

She gave him a curious look. "You and Desiree are old friends?"

He smiled. "That's strange to you, isn't it?"

"I didn't say that."

"You didn't have to. What's so weird about me being friends with Desiree?"

She shrugged. "I don't know. You just don't seem like someone who would hang with somebody like Desiree."

"Why not?" he asked, knowing the answer, but making her say it out loud. Desiree was a beautiful, artistic, unique black woman who looked like she belonged on a Paris runway, and Ryder was a nerdy white guy who studied fish.

"I don't know. You and Desiree are kind of different."

"In what ways?"

She pursed her heart-shaped lips at him, tilting her head to the side. "What's the story there?" she asked, cutting through his bull.

"I went to school with Desiree, K through twelve. When you've known somebody since you were five years old, some barriers are torn down, I guess."

She considered him. "I can see that."

"What if I told you Desiree and I dated," Ryder asked, testing the waters.

Meade lifted her eyebrows. "You and Desiree?"

"I said what if."

She shook her head. "I'd think you're full of shit."

He couldn't help laughing. "It's possible."

"No it's not," Meade said with a chuckle.

"All right. Now, you're getting ready to hurt my feelings."

"I just can't picture that. Sorry."

"We did have seven minutes together in a closet once. Seventh grade Valentine's Day party at my buddy John's house."

She leaned forward, pressing her hands on the table. "You made out with Desiree?"

"Yeah, in a twelve-year-old kind of way. It was her first kiss."

She sat back in her seat. "No, it wasn't."

"Oh yes it was."

"And yours too?"

"No, it wasn't my first. I had already kissed a girl in sixth grade. What do you take me for, some kind of late bloomer?"

Meade smiled as she twirled her drink around in circles. "You had your first kiss in the sixth grade?"

"Yeah, absolutely."

"What was the situation?"

"We were on the bus."

She sat up. "You were one of those bad boys who made out with girls on the bus?"

"I don't know why you're finding this so hard to believe."

"The boys who did that sort of thing were the same ones who played football and treated girls like crap. I don't see you like that."

"I didn't play football. And I didn't treat girls like crap. So you're right about both of those things."

"Thank you."

"But it didn't stop me from spending seven minutes in the closet with Desiree."

"And she'll corroborate this?"

"I'd prefer you not bring it up, but if you did, yeah, she would. I can't imagine she's forgotten. We've joked about it here and there over the years. I'm pretty sure she still remembers."

Meade narrowed her gaze at him. "Maybe I

formed my opinion of you too quickly."

"I'm sure you did. I told you mine. Now you tell me yours."

She grinned. "What do you want to know?"

"First kiss. How old were you?"

She looked at the ceiling, squinting. "I was sixteen."

"Sweet sixteen. Nice."

"My sixteenth birthday, if you must know."

"How did it go down?"

She rubbed her forehead. "Pretty incredibly, if I'm being honest. My best friend at the time was horrified that I had not kissed anyone yet, so she made it her mission for it to happen on my sixteenth birthday. She lined up several guys. Told them it was my first kiss. I ended up having five first kisses on that one night." She held up five fingers with a giggle that had Ryder picturing her twenty years younger.

"Did any of the four who came after the first guy know they weren't your first?"

She shook her head. "They all thought they were the first one."

"That's hard-core," Ryder said, unable to control his smile and wishing he would've been one of the five.

"Quite honestly, that's when everything changed for me. I'd been such a geeky little nerd who boys ignored. Then in that one night, I understood the power of my sexuality. I hadn't known it had existed before that. My mother was this rigid, non-sexual woman. Massive stick up her butt. It's still there, actually. She's negative, controlling...everything needing to be just so. I'd spent my whole life pleasing her up to that point, and then in this one night I understood that there was more to me than my brain. It was enlightenment on a level I had never understood."

"Some sixteenth birthday," Ryder said, feeling honored that Meade had chosen him to share this part of her development with.

"My sister never forgave me. My best friend spent the night that night, and Maya came into my room wanting to know what we were laughing about. We told her, and she started crying. She said she wanted my first kiss to be special and with a boy who cared about me. She was fourteen years old at the time." Meade shook her head. "She's been overly-protective of me her whole life."

"It must be hard balancing the dynamic. You'd have to appreciate the care, but it must be smothering."

She focused on him with those intense eyes of hers. "That's exactly how it feels."

He just nodded, letting the realization sit between them for a moment, undiscussed.

He glanced at his daughter at the other end of the restaurant, laughing with the group of kids he didn't know. "I'm probably to Annabella as your sister is to you."

"It's different when it's coming from a dad who loves you."

"How so?"

"Because a girl getting love from her dad is the ultimate fulfillment."

"Are you a daddy's girl?"

She huffed. "Hardly. But in all fairness, Maya

isn't either. He's one of those dads from an older generation who's just not very involved."

"I'm probably too involved."

"As a single dad, I imagine you have to be."

"To Annabella's chagrin." He gave Meade a rueful smile and then looked over at his daughter again. "I can't imagine knowing that Annabella had kissed five different guys in one night." He looked back at Meade. "No offense."

"None taken. I imagine no father would want to hear that about his daughter."

Ryder shook his head, his brain working through the scenario. "I would want to line them all up and just start whooping ass."

Meade's eyes got big. "Wow. Nice to meet you. Where have you been?"

"I've got a rough side," Ryder said with a smile, "especially when it comes to my daughter."

"I get it. I'd do anything for my sister, as much as she makes me insane."

Annabella walked up to the table. "Dad, they're going back to Grace's house. Can I go? She's got a pool."

"What about your chicken tenders?"

"Dad, please."

Ryder let out a sigh. "Where does she live? I'll have to come get you."

"I'll text you. I might be able to get a ride home."

"Riding in a car with a teen driver? What do you take me for?"

"Dad, please. I'll be sixteen in a few months."

"Yeah, so I've got a few months to decide what I'm gonna do about all that."

She closed her eyes, desperation covering her face. But Ryder was all too aware of the theatrics of a teenage girl, so he waited her out.

"Fine. I'll text you the address when we get there. I don't know it right now."

"That's a deal, as long as she lives here on 30A somewhere."

"She does. She's right next-door to here in Alys Beach."

Meade and Ryder exchanged a look. Alys Beach was the swankiest of all the 30A towns.

"If you don't call or text me by nine o'clock, I'm going to start driving house to house, honking the horn."

"Okay," she said and headed off.

"At least you've got a night to yourself now," Meade said.

"That is true. Big night out on the town."

"What does that look like for you?"

"Usually a craft beer and mining data."

"No girlfriend to binge Netflix with?"

"Not at the moment."

"That's right. Annabella said you hadn't dated anybody in, what was it, a million years?" She gave him a smile like she had one-upped him. He was starting to crave that smile.

"I wouldn't say a million. Half a million, maybe. Seriously, I haven't dated anyone, really, since we moved here last summer. It's just been a lot, getting Annabella set up in a new school, in a new town. I've not wanted to introduce a new girlfriend to her in the middle of all this adjustment."

"How does that work?"

"What?"

"Dating with a kid at home. Do you introduce the women to Annabella?"

"I have before."

"How does that go?"

"It hasn't been fantastic. I won't lie."

"Does that factor into the relationship?"

"Yeah, definitely. But I have found that Annabella is usually right. I can sometimes be a sucker for a beautiful woman." Ryder gave Meade a smile, making sure she knew she was one of them.

She drew her lips into a little line, the side of her mouth quirking up. She had this air about her...like she took no bullshit from anybody, including him. He was becoming more and more intrigued with her by the moment.

"You can ease up with the flattery. I'm not sleeping with you."

Ryder couldn't help but chuckle. It hadn't even occurred to him that he had a shot to sleep with her tonight. "How come? What does that server have that I don't have?"

"Zero complications."

"How am I complicated?"

"How do I count the ways?"

"What if I'm only in it for a quick lay, just like you?"

"Are you?"

Ryder shrugged, playing along. "Sure."

"With no attachments?"

"Who needs attachments?"

She narrowed her gaze at him, and then their server interrupted with their food. After she left,

Ryder said, "Don't rule it out."

"I do like to keep my options open," Meade said, picking up her fork, making him wonder exactly what magic this woman could work in bed.

Chapter Three

When they finished eating, they found themselves meandering through the Rosemary Beach town square. With the cobblestone streets and brick sidewalks flanked by the brown and white architecture, Meade held her head up an inch higher, feeling a little fancy. The area had a London Tudor feel to it but with a beachy, laid back vibe.

They stopped in the Sugar Shak and Meade marveled at the confections surrounding them—everything from gummies and hard candy to chocolate bars and fancy truffles in a case. "How will I ever choose?" she asked, picking up a giant swirled lollipop.

Ryder pointed at the menu behind the counter. "Do you want some ice cream?"

She put her hand on her belly pooch. "No, I can't after that dinner. But I will get this chocolate caramel bar for later." She waggled her eyebrows at him.

"What do you crave, Ryder?"

He just looked away from her with a grin. She was trying to keep things casual here, but he was starting to become too cute to pass up.

They walked up the street, and she remembered what was ahead of them. "Do you care if we go across the street to the Hidden Lantern bookstore? I want to pick up Neil deGrasse Tyson's new book."

"We've got that at the library."

"He's my favorite. I'll hold on to this one."

"Understood."

They crossed at a crosswalk and entered one of Meade's favorite places. She inhaled a deep breath and turned to Ryder. "I love the smell of new books."

It didn't take her long to get lost in the choices, so many books calling out to her as she ran her finger along the shelf, locating the one she came in for, but being distracted by so many others. She pulled the one she wanted off the shelf and started flipping through. Ryder showed up beside her. "Did you find it?"

She looked up at him, realizing she'd already made it through three pages. "Yeah, sorry. We can go."

"No, take your time. I would certainly never want to deny you your bookstore experience."

"You can go if you need to."

"I'm good. I'm just gonna take a look at the thrillers."

Thrillers? Meade wanted to look at the thrillers.

Half an hour later, they finally made it to the sidewalk. She pointed at her car. "I'm over there."

"I'm across the street."

They walked toward her car, and she wondered if they'd just had their first date. When they got to the driver's side, she turned to him. "Thanks for dinner. It was really good."

"Thanks for the jellybeans." He pulled the package out and opened it, popping one in. "I haven't had these in years."

"Glad to give you some nostalgia."

He offered the bag to her, and she shook her head.

"Can I call you sometime?" he asked.

She let out a sigh. "I don't think you want to do that."

"Why not?"

"Because you don't seem like a one-time guy to me, and I'm definitely a one-time girl."

"What if the one time was so amazing that you decided to change your mind about me?"

She couldn't help but wonder what sex with him would be like. Sure, he was a little nerdy, but he was cute and getting cuter by the jellybean. She opened her car door. "I'll think about it."

"Then do you want my number…in case you decide in my favor?"

"I know where to find you," she said, shutting the door. He stepped aside, allowing her room to back out. She put the car in gear, giving him one last look. She realized she'd been misjudging him. She'd been thinking of him as nerdy and cute, but he was turning hot before her very eyes with his sturdy frame and chiseled jawline. She definitely needed to avoid that library for a while. He was way too tempting.

Chapter Four

Meade stood behind the bar, sneaking a chapter in. School had started so the beaches weren't as packed as they were in the heavy tourist season. There was definitely downtime, and watching the waves only interested her so much at this point.

The idea was to get a job bumming around at the beach, which she'd succeeded in doing. It'd been fun for a while, but she was growing tired of it. It was probably time to move on. She just didn't know if that move should be to Texas working on Andrew Harrington's space program or not.

A couple came up and ordered draft beers that Meade poured for them and pocketed a hefty tip. They were probably a new couple with the man trying to impress his date—Meade's favorite kind of customer. After they stepped away, she pulled out her book, but she wasn't focused on reading today.

The Clark Kent cutie had thrown her for a loop. He had some game in him that she wasn't expecting. He knew how to flirt. Since when did nerds know how to flirt? None she had ever been around did.

She couldn't believe she told him about the night of her first kisses. She expected to be talking about math all night. But she had fun with Ryder...more fun than she'd had with any easy guy she'd been with in a while.

She'd only gone because she liked Annabella. Meade felt like a teenage girl in her head half the time. That's why she connected so well with Annabella. She didn't get the opportunity to be around teenage girls very often. She had more fun doing math with Annabella than she did on most nights out on the prowl for men. Sometimes that was more work than it was worth.

Meade's phone dinged with a text from her sister.

Just checking in. Will I see you at the opening tomorrow night?

Meade had to think about what the opening was. Maya texted again.

Desiree's and Marigold's opening?

Meade rewound to the text invite she had gotten—a picture of Desiree and Marigold holding hands and jumping into a pool with the line, *Come help us take the plunge.*

According to the invite, the two women were getting a storefront for their art business. Desiree was the artist and Marigold was the agent. Several other artists' names were featured. The showing Meade had attended at the fancy house in Alys Beach had displayed only Desiree's work. But it looked like the women were expanding their business to include others.

One art showing a year was plenty for Meade. But she did like a good party, and she could think of one nerdy New Orleans guy who she might bump into there.

She should not be thinking of that guy. He wasn't the kind of guy she wanted to get involved with. Sure, he was cute enough, but he had a whole situation going on with his daughter and his easy way of pulling Meade in. She wasn't sure what she was planning to do with her life. But she knew she was not going to be a mother this year or any other year. She needed to be able to pack her bags and go somewhere else at any moment. She was here now to take care of her sister.

Maya had been trying to have a baby unsuccessfully for a while now, which included more than one miscarriage. The latest news was that Shayla, her sister-in-law, was pregnant. Maya claimed to be really happy for them and thrilled about being an aunt, but Meade knew the news was a devastating blow to her. Meade supposed the picture she painted of Maya to Ryder had some holes in it. But Ryder didn't need to know all of her family's business. It wasn't like she was planning on hanging with him again.

Meade pocketed her phone as a group came up to the bar. She mixed Mai Tais and blended daiquiris for them, the whirl of the blender buzzing through the space around her.

The couple Meade was serving took their drinks and stepped aside, revealing the teenage girl from last night, Grace. Funny how these girls never changed. The clothes evolved, the hairdos, the technology they carried, but girls like Grace never changed. Pretty enough, even more confident, full of swagger and superiority. Meade knew her type all too well. Meade had spent her high school years hating her own brain, wishing she could be like Grace. What a waste of time that was.

"It's Meade, right?" the girl asked.

Meade was this close to saying, *No, it's Ms. Forbes*. "That's my name." Meade mirrored the girl's superior expression.

"You're like…with Annabella's dad or something?"

Meade didn't want to set that rumor into motion, but she certainly wasn't going to counter anything Annabella had told this girl. Annabella had her reasons. Meade glanced at her phone for the time. "Aren't you supposed to be in school?"

"I have study time last period."

"Ah," Meade said, because of course this girl wouldn't actually study with that time. "Would you like to order a drink?"

"Sure. Margarita."

"Not really the best drink if you don't have tequila in it."

"Who said I wouldn't have tequila in it?"

"I said it."

"Guess you're not as cool as Annabella says you are."

"Nice try with the Jedi mind tricks. If memory serves, you're a diet soda kind of girl." Meade got a cup and filled it with ice.

"I'll take a fruit tea today. I'm splurging."

Meade glanced at the girl's size double zero frame. "Splurging is good. I do it often." Meade pulled the mixture from the fridge below.

"I'm sure you have appearances to keep up here, but I'm thinking you'd have no problem getting us a few bottles of liquor for a party I'm having this weekend. I'll make it worth your while."

Meade scoffed as she handed the girl her drink. "I think I'll pass."

"You haven't heard what the currency is."

"Don't think I care."

"Something much better than money."

Meade lifted her eyebrows.

"A favor. Any favor you choose anytime you want it."

Meade supposed a girl with enough money to live in Alys Beach could provide a pretty amazing favor. "Tempting."

The girl waggled her eyebrows. "Three bottles for one big favor."

"Not in this lifetime. I'm not fond of jail cells."

Grace looked Meade up and down. "I knew you weren't as cool as Annabella made you out to be." The girl walked away. Meade huffed a laugh. Annabella thought Meade was cool, huh? That kind of made her day.

Walking into Desiree's and Marigold's opening, Meade spotted all the usual suspects in Maya's friend group. They had welcomed her in with open arms, sending her invites to all their gatherings. Her favorite was Marigold. If Meade had hooked up with Marigold before she found Dane, the two of them could've done some damage at the clubs. Marigold seemed like the kind of girl who would have been up for pretty much anything before she was tied down by a handsome and loving man.

The men in this friend group were hot as blazes, Maya's husband Bo being the hottest. Bo would jump into a volcano if Maya asked him to. He'd do anything she ever wanted or needed, and he'd probably do anything Meade asked him to by extension. Maya had hit the jackpot. Funny thing was, as fantastic and hot as Bo was, the idea of being tied down, even to someone like him, made Meade's skin crawl.

She'd done the whole unhealthy relationship thing with a handful of guys she fell for hard and fast, but she'd learned from those mistakes and was happily moving on to a less erratic life…one that included remaining single and working on herself.

Now that she'd scrubbed that toxicity out of her life, what she valued more than anything was her freedom. The idea of being suffocated by a man on the couch watching Netflix every night made her itchy.

"I love this dress," Marigold said by way of greeting, checking Meade out.

"Look at you," Meade said, motioning at Marigold. "Nobody else can pull off that purple like you."

Marigold leaned in. "So, what's happening? Tell me about your latest flings. I love to live vicariously through you."

"Oh, please. Like you're not with the hottest twin in Florida." Dane had a twin brother, Ethan, who was somehow even better looking than he was. Ethan's boyfriend, Ashe, was one of the only men who could make Meade blush. Maya had said he had an Adam Lambert thing going on, but Meade thought it was more like a Brendon Urie thing from Panic! At the Disco. Either way, Meade could totally get on board with that sort of sophisticated glam rock look. But alas, he was gay and taken. Double whammy.

Marigold glanced over at her man, who was standing with his twin brother and the hot Ashe, who sported guyliner making Meade drool a little. Yummy.

The men walked their way, and hugs were given all around. "You three look like you're ready to break some hearts," Meade said.

"You're working the hell out of that dress," Ashe said.

Meade's cheeks went hot as she moved her hands over her hips. "Thank you. I knew this group would be dressed to the nines."

"Yeah, but you're a ten," Ethan said with a wink.

Damn, Meade loved gay men.

Ashe pulled her aside. "Who's the guy?"

"What do you mean?" Meade asked him, trying to look innocent.

"I know women. You don't wear dresses like that unless there's a man involved." He looked around the room. "Who is he?"

Meade's gaze landed on Ryder, who stood across the room looking handsome in his shirt and tie, his shaggy hair tamed for the moment. She almost didn't recognize him at first glance without his cute little glasses on. He was talking to a woman Meade didn't recognize. She hated that a flash of jealousy moved through her.

"I'm dressed like this for you. Hoping I can get you and your boyfriend to try me out for a night."

"Bullshit." His gaze zoned in on her. She glanced at Ryder again and then took a sip of her wine.

Ashe's gaze drew to Ryder. "Ryder?"

Meade should've known Ashe would know him. Desiree and Ashe were attached at the hip.

"No," Meade said with a chuckle, like it was the most ridiculous idea ever.

Ashe looked like his wheels were turning. "Why not him?"

"He's a marine biologist."

"What does that have to do with anything?"

"I don't date guys like that."

"What kind of guys do you date?"

"Easy ones. That one has a fifteen-year-old daughter going on twenty-one. No thanks."

They both stepped out of the way of a dessert cart being rolled past them full of delights Meade would have to check out in a bit.

"I do understand that," Ashe said. "I'm not gonna be anyone's daddy anytime soon."

"Are you sure about that? You and Ethan aren't talking kids?"

"Not our thing. And quit turning this around on me."

Meade rolled her eyes.

"Oh, look. He knows we're talking about him," Ashe said.

Meade looked at Ryder, and he gave her a knowing smile. "Shit," Meade said under her breath. She smiled and waved. "You're going to get me in trouble."

"Or maybe a date," Ashe said, waving Ryder over.

Ryder walked their way, and Meade greeted him with a courteous smile, trying to save face.

"Hello, my friend," Ashe said, giving Ryder a hug.

"What's up with you?" Ryder asked Ashe. "Last time I talked to you, you were photographing the first family, right?"

Ashe laughed. "That or some tourists with plenty of cash. Either works for me." Ashe slid his gaze to Meade and then back to Ryder. "So, the two of you have met?" Ashe's dark eyebrow rose.

"A couple of times now," Ryder said, meeting Meade's gaze, quickening her heartbeat with his rich, dark eyes. Damn, he was getting hotter by the day.

"The two brainiacs of our group interacting. Everyone, hold onto your hats," Ashe said.

Meade gave him a look. There was nothing she hated more than someone pointing out how smart she was. Ever since high school she'd worked to conceal her thirst for knowledge, but there was no hiding it when her sister was constantly telling everyone how brilliant Meade was. She would be flattered if she didn't know that Maya was just doing it because she was ashamed of Meade and her life choices.

"Don't lump me into that duo," Ryder said. "I don't think I could keep up with her."

"Where's Annabella tonight?" Meade asked, desperate to change the subject.

"Out with friends. She's staying the night with that kid, Grace, we met the other night."

"Uh-oh," Ashe said. "By the look on your face, this isn't a love connection?"

"The girl's just a little advanced for fifteen," Ryder said, looking at Meade for confirmation.

She thought about the girl trying to get a drink off of her and have Meade buy liquor for her at the bar earlier in the week. But Meade wasn't about to confirm or deny anything and trip Annabella up. If this was the girl she wanted to be around these days, Meade wasn't there to judge or impede upon that.

Someone Meade didn't recognize walked up to Ashe. "There's an engaged couple over here I want to introduce you to. Potential new client with big bucks."

Ashe waggled his eyebrows at Meade and Ryder. "I'm always up for one of those. You two talk amongst yourselves." He winked and then made his exit.

Ryder narrowed his gaze at Meade, wordlessly, and she broke into a smile, unable to help herself.

"What?" he said, smiling with just one side of his mouth.

"Nothing. I almost didn't recognize you without your glasses."

"Ah, yes. I ditched them for tonight." He leaned in. "I have a secret I kind of wanna tell you."

Meade tried to move from uncontrollable smile mode back to cool flirtatious mode. "I love secrets."

"I wondered if you'd be here."

Meade tried not to let her girl parts rattle. "That's a terrible secret."

"Why would you say that?"

"I thought you were going to tell me something juicy."

"I can make something up if you'd prefer."

"You better come up with something good or I'm walking."

"Pressure's on, isn't it?" He scrubbed his hands together. "Let's see. I think the secret is… I kind of like you."

She tried so hard to wipe the stupid grin off her face. "If you're trying to land me in your bed, you're going to have to do better than that."

"You heard me say my daughter was out, didn't you?"

"Logistics? That's how you're trying to reel me in?"

"Logistics are big for a single dad."

"There's never any kids at my place, so logistics are never our problem."

"Then what could possibly be standing in our way?"

35

Meade just shook her head, glancing around the room. She spotted her sister talking with a tall, handsome man in a thousand-dollar suit. Maya caught sight of Meade, doing a double take, her eyes going wide. She glanced back at the guy, letting him finish his sentence, seeming desperate for him to shut up.

"Oh shit," Meade said.

"That didn't sound good. What's up?"

"My sister."

"Where is she?"

"Over there with the light blond hair. Looks like she lives on a running track."

"I believe I've met her."

"I'm sure you have if you've been around this group. And you're getting ready to be re-introduced. She's just dying for that guy to shut up so she can bring him over here."

"She likes to set you up?"

"Trust me, this isn't a romantic set up. A hundred bucks says this guy is CEO of somewhere and she thinks he's going to hire me."

"She sets you up with business contacts?"

"She's been known to. Here we go," Meade said, noticing Maya pointing and the man turning to look with stars in his eyes and a smile.

"You must be super qualified for something," Ryder said. "He looks like he's about to hire Bill Gates."

"How are you at playing along?"

"I've been known to try improv. But warning, the stint was short-lived."

Meade plastered on a tempered smile as Maya approached with the man. "Meade, I'd like to introduce you to…" She lost her laser focus for a second as she glanced at Ryder. "We've met, right?"

"I believe so. Ryder. I'm Meade's new employer."

Meade may have fallen a little in love with Ryder at

that moment.

Maya blinked. "You are? I thought you were a marine biologist?"

"By day. I'm a neuro physicist by night. Meade is working on a study with me about the brain. We're digging in to see if there's a new laser that could target amoeba and protons in the esophageal node."

Meade fought hard to tamp down her urge to laugh.

Maya gave Meade a warning glance. "Meade," she said through gritted teeth, "I'd like you to meet David Alastair. He's a professor at Florida Midwest University. He's in the history department. He focuses on American history. He says there's an opening for a faculty position assisting in women's historical studies."

"How fabulous," Meade said, shaking his hand and holding eye contact. She ran her thumb over his knuckle just to mess with him.

He cleared his throat, looking to be recalibrating his approach. "Maya said you're a history buff. She said you've read every book on important women in American history."

Meade raised an eyebrow. "Now David, aren't all women important?"

"Well, of course, but surely you agree that some women have made groundbreaking strides in our country's progress."

"Yes, but I think Sheila who does my nails has taken manicures to the next level. Look at this shade. She created this color herself. Have you ever seen such a vibrant violet?" Meade wiggled her manicure in front of her chest.

The guy just stood there, narrowing his gaze at her hand.

"I can't believe I have been here all of fifteen minutes and still have not gotten a cocktail." Meade turned to Ryder. "We should probably do something about that, shouldn't we?"

"Definitely," Ryder said.

"David, it's been a pleasure," Meade said taking his hand and shaking it, cupping her other hand over the top of it. Poor guy couldn't tell whether to be offended or ask for her number.

Meade took Ryder's arm and let him lead her toward the bar.

"Actually," she said as they were about to get in line, "if you don't get me out of here right now, I may die of boredom."

"That sounds tragic."

She just raised her eyebrow at him.

He shrugged. "Let's go."

Chapter Five

Ryder could not muck up this opportunity. Meade was bored and counting on him to show her a good time. Sure, she just wanted to get away from her sister and the perfectly pleasant man who she just took down to his knees. Ryder shouldn't admit how much fun he had watching that, by the way.

But Meade was not ready to let him in yet, emotionally or physically. This was his chance to make strides. Logistics were on his side. His daughter was taken care of for the night. He just had to think of something good...and quick.

Meade looked at her phone, tossing it into her purse where she came up with keys. She flipped back her short, blond curls. Her hair reminded him of a style he'd seen in a Marilyn Monroe picture. In fact, her body was Monroe-esque, especially in that fitted dress that showed her generous cleavage. He'd seen her dressed up twice now, and both times he'd thought she was one of the most exquisite beauties he'd seen in a long time. "I think I'll head home and check out this new documentary on poisoned rivers," she said.

"Don't," Ryder said, his voice coming off like a command. He was about to apologize when he saw something flicker in her eyes. Interest? "I want to show you something."

She narrowed her gaze. "Where?"

"At the marina where I do my fieldwork."

She shrugged. "As long as it's better than poisoned rivers."

"I think it will be."

They walked to his car, and he opened the door for her, letting her in. As he got in the driver's seat, she said, "It's been a while since someone's done that for me."

"Do the young guys you date not open your door?"

"Not all the guys I date are young. Some are just older guys who aren't complicated."

"What's so complicated about me?"

"You know," she said.

He shook his head as he drove them down Highway 30A toward the marina. When they got there, he tried not to let his stomach get nervous. This was his domain. He spent a lot of his days in front of the computer mining data, but this was where he came to get his hands wet.

"Is this your boat?" she asked as they approached the dock.

"It belongs to the private company I work for."

"Dang," she said. "I thought it would be a little more bare-bones than this."

"That's the advantage of working for a private company. If I was working for a nonprofit, it might be a different story."

She gave him a curious look. "I'm sort of surprised you work for a private company. You definitely strike me as a nonprofit type."

He faked plunging a knife in his chest. "I don't know

if that was supposed to be an insult or not, but it felt like one."

She gave him a smile. "You just seem kind of earthy."

"Do you mean poor?"

"I did not say that," she said with her eyebrows up.

"It's okay. Marine biologists aren't hedge fund operators, but we do okay."

"I'm sure you do. Your work seems interesting enough if this is where you come to do it every day."

He stepped onto the boat and then helped her on. "In full disclosure, I don't come here every day. A lot of my work is done on my laptop. Enough data to make your eyes cross."

"How often do you get out here?"

"As much as I can justify it. I really like to be in the ocean."

"I assume you scuba dive and all of that?" she asked.

"I wouldn't be proud to call myself a marine biologist if I didn't know how to scuba dive. Do you know how?"

"No, I'm more of a reader than a doer."

"Maybe we can change that."

"Oh no. You're not getting me in one of those suits."

"What about snorkeling? How do you feel about that?"

She shrugged. "I don't know. Never tried."

"No suit involved in that. Just a mask."

"Let me think about it," she said, walking away from him and inspecting the boat.

Ryder didn't think he'd ever known a woman more in control of herself than Meade. She was cool and self-assured like no woman he'd ever attempted to date. Admittedly, he'd never tried to date a woman like Meade before. The women he typically went out with enjoyed science and reading. That was the reason he felt comfortable enough to approach Meade. He'd had a gander at her reading material at the library. Without that, he never would've thought to go for her.

Meade had an edge that the women he usually dated didn't have. He had never tried so openly to get a woman in his bed. That was something he always tiptoed around, working on building trust within his relationships so that one day he could work up to sex. But Meade tended to bring out his alpha side. He kind of liked it.

She walked around the deck to the front of the boat and put her hands on the railing. "Nice," she said, looking out into the ocean.

"Do you love the beach?" he asked.

"So much that I got a job working on one. We were landlocked growing up. We didn't get to the beach too much. I figured with my sister living here, now was the perfect time to get my fill."

"Sounds like an opportunity."

"It was, but I'm not sure how long it'll last."

"Oh," he said, trying not to let his heart break a little.

"You saw how she was tonight. My sister and I are great together as long as we're at least a few states apart." She turned around, resting against the railing.

"May I ask an intrusive question?"

She raised one eyebrow.

"Why don't you want to work for that guy?"

She rolled her eyes and turned back around, gripping the railing. "I've done that. It's not for me."

"What exactly is not for you?"

"Academia, the corporate world, it's all the same."

Ryder tossed up his hands. "Look at me. I'm not in the corporate world."

"You said you worked for a private business."

"True, but I get to dive into the ocean from time to time and get paid for it. Have you ever thought about marine biology?"

She glanced around, agitation clear on her face. "Do you have anything to drink on this boat?"

"Anything you want." He led her inside and walked to

42

the bar.

"Wow," she said, glancing around the entertainment area. "This is pretty cushy for a work boat."

"We host people on here sometimes. Donors, corporate execs. It's a multi-use boat. What's your drink?"

"I'm not picky. Surprise me," she said, taking a seat and running her hand across the leather.

He joined her on the couch, handing her the vodka drink. She took a sip. "I like this. Just sweet enough."

He loved how every phrase she uttered seemed to have a double meaning. Or maybe it was just the way she looked at him like the cat who caught the canary. She was so good at the flirting game. He was just trying to keep up. "What did you go to school for?" he asked.

She waved him off, taking a sip of her drink.

"You can share that side of yourself with me, you know."

"I don't know about that," she said.

"Why wouldn't you be able to?"

She looked away from him, and then stared down at her drink a minute like she was considering something. "I went for prelaw."

"Did you go to law school after that?"

"I did."

"Did you ever practice?"

"For about two seconds. It wasn't what I wanted to do. I was just following the plan my parents had mapped out for me. My dad is an attorney and my mom was his paralegal. It was always assumed I would be a lawyer. I just rolled with it for lack of really knowing what I wanted to do with my life."

"What did you quit law to do?"

She chuckled. "I worked on a cruise ship for a few months."

"How did that come about?"

"This girl I met at a bar one night was doing it and told me all about it. I thought it sounded like fun."

He was caught between being mortified that she'd quit a job at a law firm to work on a cruise ship, and being impressed at the guts it must have taken to walk away from a lawyer's life. "Was it fun?"

"For a bit. Then like anything else, it got old."

"What kind of law did you practice?"

"Tax law."

"I've heard that's one of the most difficult kinds to practice. Would you say so?"

"I don't know if I would call it difficult. It's just constantly reading the new IRS regulations that come out. I did it for a while, and then I realized I would much rather be reading about the universe or the women's suffrage movement." She shrugged. "Law just wasn't for me."

"Then why not make a career out of astrophysics or politics?"

She shifted in her seat, her face flushing. "I did work in astrophysics for a while. It wasn't for me."

"But bartending is?"

"I don't know why this has to be a thing. People work as bartenders. They work on cruise ships. Why can't I be one of those people?"

"It looks like you are one of those people."

"Why can't I do it without judgment?"

"I'm not judging you. I'm just trying to understand where you're coming from."

She gazed into his eyes, looking like she was gauging him. "What if I sound like an asshole if I tell you the truth?"

"Like I said, this is a judgment-free zone."

She stared at him for a long while and then finally said, "They want too much from me, whether it's working for a law firm or for the government with top-secret clearance. I keep taking these jobs thinking this is going to be the one where I can settle in and enjoy the work at my own pace and on my own level. But I research whatever project I'm given and present results, and then these people act like I fucking unlocked the secret to life. They always bring me in for serious discussions with upper-level personnel and tell me they want me running departments and watching over people who are twice my age who have been at it for thirty or forty years. Everyone starts eyeing me like I'm out to get them. They all get paranoid I'm trying to outperform them or take their job. I just want to work and go home. That's it. I don't want to participate in all this competition. I've never been a competitor."

He wondered if she didn't care for competition because she was always the best naturally, but he kept his comments to himself. "How did you get the job in astrophysics?"

She shook her head like it was insignificant. "Connections. I wrote a thesis paper and got a professor to read it. It sort of took on a life of its own."

"You mean you wrote a thesis paper on something in astrophysics without having studied it in college?"

"Yeah," she said, glancing around like she was bored.

"And it was impressive enough to have the professor connect you with a job?"

She started to stand up. "This is making me uncomfortable. I'd like to go."

He put his hand on her arm. "I didn't mean anything by that. I'm just feeling my way around here, okay?" The way she looked at him, he could tell her sister had probably gotten the same look a million times. "You're a puzzle, Meade. You're an interesting as hell puzzle. I'm just trying to put the pieces together."

"Believe me, you're never gonna solve that puzzle, because there's a few missing pieces."

"What are those?"

She took a deep breath and then let it out as if she had been holding it for years. "If I knew, do you think I'd be working at a bar on the beach?"

He didn't know how to solve her equation, so he searched for anything he knew. "What about being a parent? Is that something you've thought about? I know you said that wasn't for you, but really, have you thought about it? It changes people's lives. I can attest to that."

"That's not it. I've never wanted to be a mother, not even when I was little. I had no baby dolls."

"What did you have?"

She gave him a smirk. "What do you think I had?"

He thought about it, wanting to get this right. "Robots."

She smiled. "Transformers. A ton of them."

He'd never been so proud of himself for getting a test question right. He gauged her, working her out. "What's funny is, you don't seem to be looking for anything."

She shook her head. "I'm not."

"I can't process that. Everybody's looking for something—happiness in lottery tickets or parenthood, a relationship. People are always trying to do something. You seem okay to just be."

"Who said I'm okay?"

They studied each other for a minute. He was afraid to speak. With the way she was looking at him, he had the feeling not too many people were let into Meade's brain like this.

"Screw it. I'm fine. Just irritated with my sister. And I guess I feel a little bad for what I did to that guy back there."

"I think he'll survive it."

"Thank you for jumping in, by the way."

"No problem. I was good as long as she wasn't trying to set you up on a date with him."

She shook her head, staring off into the middle

distance. "You don't want to get mixed up with me, Ryder. I'm a hot mess."

"You don't look very messy from where I'm sitting."

She grinned at him. "You have a line or two in you, don't you?"

"I've got a whole slew of them."

"I'm not sure you're what I thought you were."

He chuckled. "Is that good or bad?"

"I don't know yet. It could be dangerous."

He was this close to saying danger was his middle name, then he realized that was a nerd thing to say. He was going for Alpha. "You look like a girl who could use some danger."

She giggled, and he knew he screwed it up. He got even cheesier than he originally thought to. He had to recover.

"Do you want to skinny dip with the sharks?" he asked.

She gave him that lazy gaze. "Have you ever been skinny-dipping in the ocean?"

Just the idea of it made him want to cover his balls. "No, but I have been skinny-dipping in a swimming pool. What are the chances of getting you to do that with me?"

"Skinny-dipping is overrated," she said like she'd done it a million times.

"Then how about we do the skinny-dipping without the water?"

She squinted at him. "I'm having trouble getting a read on you. If I were to take you up on any one of these advances, would you actually follow through?"

"This feels a little like a dare," he said, sensing the moment intensifying.

She shrugged. "Call it whatever you want. Just make sure you understand the shark you're skinny-dipping with here, Ryder."

Every time she said his name, he felt like melting into

an unidentified mass.

"Noted."

There was only one thing left to do, and if he waited a second longer, he'd miss the opportunity, so he leaned in.

Chapter Six

Meade could not believe she was encouraging this guy, but she'd pushed the door wide open, and he was walking through it. His lips landed on hers, giving her torso a shock of electricity. Damn. She was not expecting him to be a good kisser, but he somehow knew exactly what he was doing. He took the kiss slow but let her know he was in charge, careful not to elevate things too quickly.

Just as she felt his hand moving up her thigh, their mouths opened, and holy shit. It'd been a minute since Meade had experienced a first kiss, and definitely longer than that since she'd had one with this kind of sexual tension. She'd had her fair share of one-night stands, but they were more get-to-the-point with way less danger involved. She'd had her heart broken just last year, as a matter of fact, in Las Vegas. She found a couple of recovery guys to ease her pain, but none who came with the kinds of attachments that Ryder had.

His thumb swept over her inner thigh, and she warmed to him. She had been talking a big game, telling him he needed to understand her rules, but she needed to repeat those rules to herself. No attachments. No long-term relationships. No fifteen-year-old insta-daughters. Meade would do fine helping Annabella with math and letting that be the end of it. She was nobody's mother, and she refused to play the role of one.

She pulled away, running her finger over her lips. "Not bad."

"Not at all."

She stood. "I need to get out of here before we end up doing something stupid."

"I think what we're doing is pretty damn brilliant."

She turned and headed toward the door before he tried to kiss her again...or before she found herself jumping his bones.

"I'll be out in a second. I'm just gonna put these glasses away," he said.

"Mmm," she uttered, and then waited for him outside, giving herself an internal pep talk.

Do not go home with this man. Do not sleep with him. He will suck you in. You don't want a daughter, and you don't want someone who will make you feel like you can't be yourself. He'll never be satisfied with you working as a bartender or a blackjack dealer, or anything else you choose. He'll constantly be wanting to bring you into science. You're not gonna let that happen.

He came outside, locking the door behind him. "You ready?"

"Yep," she said and followed him to his car. He opened the door for her again and she got inside, trying to imagine the last time that Max from Vegas had opened the door for her. He'd done it once the very first night they were to sleep together. Then he never did it again. He also never went to work again. Meade had spent the next few months dealing cards and supporting his worthless ass. But this is the kind of shit Meade pulled. She fell for bad guys and completely lost her sense of self.

Ryder was a good guy. She didn't want to put him through her psychosis. She wasn't happy without chaos, and she had to figure out the root of that before she allowed a good guy into her heart. In the meantime, she just wanted to be left alone and live an easy life with simple men who wanted nothing more from her than a good time.

"You seem deep in thought," Ryder said, waking Meade back to reality.

"Sorry," she said, adjusting herself in her seat. "Just thinking about another life."

"Want to tell me about it?"

She gave a humorless laugh. "Not at all."

"Something bad?"

"Not bad, just stupid on my part."

"It's hard for me to imagine a woman as smart as you are doing much of anything that's stupid."

"There's a big difference between book smarts and relationship smarts."

"What was your last relationship like?"

She shook her head in disgust. "A disaster."

"Young guy?" he asked.

"He was close to my age. Just not very good for me."

"Tell me about it."

"Tell me about your latest relationship," she said.

"Turning the tables, huh?"

"You tell me yours and I'll tell you mine."

He re-gripped the steering wheel. "That's fair enough. Her name was Elise. She was a kindergarten teacher."

Meade couldn't imagine anyone better for Ryder than a kindergarten teacher. "How did you meet her?"

"It was a set up through friends."

"And it worked out?" she asked. "Set ups never work out."

"I've had a few work out, for a while at least."

51

She adjusted the strap of her seatbelt. "I stand corrected. Set ups never work out for me. Go ahead."

He let out a deep breath. "It lasted about seven months."

"How did it go with Annabella?"

"Annabella didn't love her, but she didn't hate her either."

"That's probably more than you can ask for."

"Probably."

"What ended it?"

He shrugged. "I don't know. It just wasn't there for me. For a long time, I thought I needed to find a mom for her. I thought Elise would be good in that role. She was desperate for kids and very interested in Annabella's life. I sat down with Annabella before I made any decisions and had a talk with her about it. She had no problem with me breaking up with Elise. Said she just wanted me to be happy and if she wasn't the right person, then she thought I should let her go."

"How did Elise take it?" Meade could hear the jealousy in her own tone when she said the woman's name.

"Not well. She thought I was getting ready to propose. She wanted to be married so badly. I think that was part of the problem. It was just a lot of pressure. We were considering moving here, and it just seemed like a do or die moment."

"And you weren't ready to die?"

He huffed a laugh. "I was going to say I wasn't ready to do. But yeah, I guess that could be interpreted either way. Also, she wanted kids. I've already had my kid. I'm okay to have more, but it's not something I'm actively pursuing."

"I would think kids would be an all-or-nothing kind of thing. Either you're actively pursuing them, or you're not interested."

He shrugged. "I try to roll with things in life. I guess when you have an unplanned pregnancy, you're forced to learn how to roll with things."

She considered him. "Do you want to tell me about Annabella's mom?"

"I think I told you she's not in her life."

"What life is she in?"

He shook his head, his eyes focused on the road. "I honestly don't even know."

"Were you guys high school sweethearts?"

"College sweethearts. We found out we were pregnant a week before graduation. She'd been offered a job with a nonprofit working in shark science. It'd been all she'd wanted to do since she was a little girl. The job required a lot of travel, a lot of hard work, and it didn't allow a lot of time for infants."

"Did she consider abortion?"

"It wasn't an option for her. She's Catholic and her family is very religious. She hid the pregnancy from her employer for as long as she could. By the time she started showing and had to fess up, they couldn't fire her."

"I would hope not."

"The plan was to give Annabella up for adoption."

"How did you feel about that?"

"I'm ashamed to say I considered it. In fact, I was pretty sure I was going to follow through with it if it weren't for my mother. She was so happy about the pregnancy. My father had been dead since I was two, and she had been so lonely since I'd left the house for college. She begged me to keep Annabella. She said she would raise her and I could be as involved as I wanted."

"What happened there?"

"When Annabella was three, my mother developed cancer in her lymph nodes."

"I'm so sorry."

He shrugged. "Like I say, in life you have to roll with

things and make adjustments. That's why I'm open to more kids or not. I just kind of take what life throws at me."

She wanted desperately to reach over and touch his arm for comfort, but she could feel herself getting sucked into the vortex.

"Should I drop you off at the restaurant?" he asked.

"Actually, I took a ride share there. You can just drop me at home."

"Where is home?"

"Around the corner from Rosemary Beach off 98. I rent a converted garage."

"How did you find that?"

"Facebook. The woman who I rent from travels a lot. She's been out of town for a few months now. She likes me watching over the place."

"Does she rent it out to tourists?"

"No, it's not that kind of place. Since it's off the highway, it's not really beachy. That's why I have to work at the beach, to get my fill." She gave him a wink.

Meade directed him to the house and he pulled into the driveway. "Let me walk you to the door," he said, attempting to get out of the car.

She put her hand on his arm. "Don't you dare."

He grinned. "I promise I wasn't planning on trying to get in there."

"I can't promise that back. That's why I need you to stay in the car."

He let out a sigh, resigning himself. "What if I'm as big of a mess as you are?"

"I don't think so," she said, calling his bullshit.

"I don't know what the hell I'm doing with my fifteen-year-old daughter. She's going to turn sixteen soon and I'll have to hand her a set of keys to the car. Don't think I'm not freaking out about that."

"She's going to be just fine."

"Easy for you to say. You're not the one who'll be waiting up till two in the morning."

"Two? That's some curfew."

"Curfew's eleven."

"Has she broken it before?"

"Not yet, but I've got my eye on this new friend of hers."

She nodded without hesitation.

"Did you get the same vibe?" he asked.

"Oh, no," she said, hoping he couldn't tell she was lying.

"You do, don't you?"

"I know everything about her that you know. Nothing more." She hoped he couldn't tell her ears were burning, something that happened when she lied.

"Fair enough." Meade tried to get out of the car, and Ryder said, "You didn't tell me your relationship story yet."

"Next time," she said.

"I'm gonna take you up on that. How about tomorrow night?"

She smiled at him, shaking her head. "You don't give up easily, do you?"

"Not after that kiss."

Man, she wanted to let him come in.

"Are you working tomorrow night?" he asked.

"I work Monday through Friday. A college kid takes my post on the weekends."

"Then you're free tomorrow night?"

"I never said I was free. What if I have a date?"

"Do you have a date?"

"Possibly. David Alastair slipped me his number earlier."

This made him smile. "How about I pick you up at six?"

"To do what?"

55

"Dinner?"

"What about Annabella? Will she be joining us?"

"She's fifteen. She can stay at home by herself."

"Now I'm feeling guilty."

"Guilty enough to take advantage of her spending the night away tonight and let me come in?"

Meade was gonna have to do something about the permanent smile he was leaving on her face.

"I am not sleeping with you due to a set of favorable logistics."

"I understand that. Let me worry about my daughter. You just be ready for me to pick you up at six o'clock tomorrow."

"Aye aye, captain." She got out of the car, wondering what in the world she was getting herself into with him.

Chapter Seven

As Ryder got ready for his date with Meade, he kept an eye on his daughter who had been sullen and had her head buried in her phone all day. This wasn't unusual for her, but today felt different.

"You sure you're okay to hang here by yourself?"

She waved him off distractedly.

"Any chance you'll tell me what might be going on with you today?"

She let out the sigh to end all sighs. "I just don't know what I've done wrong. Everything went great last night but Grace has not reached out to me today. We're supposed to be hanging this evening."

This was news to him. She was still fifteen and needed him to cart her around. But leave it to a teenager to not consider those kinds of insignificant details.

"Did you try texting her?"

"Yes, like two hours ago. She hasn't responded yet."

"Why don't you call her?"

Annabella just looked at him like he was the biggest

moron on the planet.

He sat down with her. "I don't have to go, you know. I can stay here and we can pop some popcorn and find a movie."

Her shoulders sagged like that was the worst idea she'd ever heard. "I guess."

His heart sank because he really did want to see Meade. But this was his daughter and he needed to be there for her. "Okay, let me cancel my plans."

He called Meade and she answered, her voice smooth as silk as she said, "You better not be canceling."

"I'm so sorry."

"Wait, who is that?" Annabella asked. "Is that Meade?"

He loosely covered the receiver. "Yes, give me just a minute."

"Let me talk to her."

"Annabella, please. Just give me a minute."

"I want to talk to her."

"Just put me on the phone with her," Meade said.

Ryder sat there looking at Annabella. Meade had been crystal clear that she did not want to be a mother. He didn't want to drag her into anything she didn't want to be a part of.

"Ryder," Meade said, "let me talk to Annabella."

"Okay," he said, handing the phone to his daughter with hesitancy.

She snatched it from him. "Hey, can you come over?"

Annabella stood up and walked away from him. "My dad and I are having movie night. Do you wanna join us? We can get a raunchy girl movie."

Jesus. Now Meade was going to think that he never even planned to see her the way Annabella was describing the evening to her.

"Okay, cool. We've got stuff to make cookies, if you want to do that." Annabella walked away, cupping her mouth as she talked so Ryder couldn't hear. A couple of minutes later, she emerged from her room giggling. It was amazing how much her mood had lifted in the seconds she had gotten on the phone with Meade. "Okay, here's my dad."

Ryder took the phone, walking onto the deck. "I'm so sorry. I hope you know I really did plan for us to go out tonight."

"It's fine," Meade said.

"The way she described it to you, she and I had this planned all along, but what happened was—"

"Ryder, I've been a fifteen-year-old girl. I know the drill. What's your address?"

"Can I come and get you?"

"I'm good to drive."

He gave her the address. "And thank you for this. You don't have to—"

"See you in a few."

When the bell rang, Annabella jumped up and rushed to the door. Ryder walked up behind her, seeing Meade in the doorway in shorts and a T-shirt with a girl group on the front called The Donnas, wiggling a DVD with Cameron Diaz on the cover. "This is the one that got the raunchy girl movies started. Can you handle it?"

His daughter grabbed the movie. "Awesome. I love Cameron Diaz."

Meade met Ryder's gaze and winced. "I just realized that might be rated R."

He shrugged. "She's about to be sixteen. I've got to let go at some point."

"Let's make the cookies," Annabella said.

Ryder gave Meade a look. "You don't have to make cookies with Annabella."

"I am fine with making cookies as long as I get to eat them when we're done." Meade headed into the kitchen.

"I hope you've got a recipe pulled up because I have no clue how to make cookies."

Ryder ran a hand through his hair. He felt trapped. His daughter seemed to be connecting with the only woman he'd dated who most definitely did not want to be a mother figure. He felt bad, but Annabella needed this, and Meade could've said she couldn't come. He decided to say screw it and just let the evening roll.

He walked into the kitchen and found them hovered over a phone, talking in hushed voices. He walked right back out and stood in his living room, feeling displaced, then went into his bedroom to get himself together. He changed into something more comfortable since Meade had dressed down. When he got back to the kitchen, the two of them were measuring white powders that looked like flour and sugar.

"Nuts or no nuts?" Annabella asked.

"Nuts, but only if we can double the chocolate chips."

Annabella grinned. "Perfect."

Ryder stood in the doorway feeling like the odd man out. "I could go get us some food. We don't really have anything here."

"Food would be good," Meade said with a smile and then went back to her bowl.

"Can we get takeout from Cowgirl Kitchen?" Annabella asked and then turned to Meade. "They have amazing tacos."

Meade turned to Ryder. "We'll have some amazing tacos, please."

"And salads," Annabella said. "Because we're watching our figures."

Meade and Annabella gave conspiratorial giggles, and Ryder turned to walk out. He couldn't believe the transformation Annabella had made. He'd never seen her like this around a woman he was dating. She was usually distrustful and skeptical. But she and Meade were making fast friends.

The more he thought about it, the more he realized this could be a mistake. What if Annabella got attached to Meade, and then Meade decided she wasn't interested in him or in being some kind of mentor or friend to his daughter? He didn't want Annabella to have to go through yet another heartbreak. The kid had it hard enough, not having a mother or grandparents. It had never been hard breaking up with women because Annabella had never been wild about anyone he dated. But there was no question that she was crazy about Meade. He grabbed his keys and walked out of the house, hoping for the best out of this evening, whatever that was.

Chapter Eight

Somehow Ryder had ended up in the armchair with Meade and Annabella curled up together on the couch, a bowl of popcorn between them. They had been snort-laughing their way through the movie. Ryder had barely paid attention. He couldn't take his eyes off of Meade and the way she was with his daughter. How did she have that knack? Especially if she wasn't wild about kids. The other women he dated had worked months, even years in a case or two, trying to work their way into Annabella's heart. Meade had done it before he and she even had their first real date.

Annabella's phone dinged and she grabbed it. "Oh my gosh, it's Grace."

"What is she saying?" Meade asked.

"She wants to know where I am. Oh my God this makes me so mad. She's acting like I should just know to be there or something when she never gave me any kind of details."

"I'm calling B.S.," Meade said.

"For sure. What do I do?"

Meade considered her and then glanced at Ryder. He just shrugged, wanting to see how Meade would suggest to play this out.

She turned back to Annabella. "Do you want to go?"

She bit her lip. "Kind of."

Meade tugged her foot up underneath her. "Say, 'Maybe we'll stop by.'"

"Who's we?"

"We'll figure that out. But this way it doesn't look like you've been sitting around waiting for her all night."

Annabella thumbed into her phone and then looked up at Meade a few seconds later when her phone dinged again. "She wants to know where I am."

"Say, 'Out with friends.'"

"She's going to ask what friends. She knows I don't have any."

"Just say it."

Annabella thumbed into her phone again. A few seconds later, she said, "She wants to know who I'm with."

"Say, 'Some friends from out of town.' That way you don't actually have to produce them."

Annabella thumbed into her phone again.

Ryder wondered if lying was really the best answer, but he'd opened himself up for this when he shrugged his approval to Meade a minute ago.

"I've got some kids who'll back us up if we get desperate," Meade said. "There's twin boys around your age who live next-door to me. We'll say it's their cousins in from out of town or something. I bet I can even get them to do a selfie with you for proof if we need it."

"Oh my God, are you serious?"

"Whatever it takes. We're not gonna let this girl think she owns you."

"Or Annabella could just find some friends who don't put her through this kind of drama," Ryder said. Both girls

63

looked at him with heads cocked to the side like a dog who heard a weird noise.

"Dad. Please."

He tossed up both hands. They waited, staring at the phone, and then Annabella said, "What now?"

"Either we can take you over there in like half an hour so you don't look desperate, or you can blow the whole thing off and make her wonder," Meade said.

Annabella whispered something to Meade, and Meade nodded as if everything made perfect sense to her now.

Meade stood up. "Let's go find something for you to wear."

Ryder twiddled his thumbs until the two girls came out of Annabella's bedroom. Annabella wore one of the short dresses that he hated the most. But he understood this was how the kids dressed these days. Annabella always told him it wasn't nearly as short as the other girls' dresses. He figured that may be the truth, but this was as short as he could stand his fifteen-year-old daughter to be seen in.

"I'll run her over there," Meade said.

"I'm coming," Ryder said, not wanting Meade to be able to drive straight home after she dropped Annabella off. It was conniving, but he needed a reason for her to come back to his house. He wanted to salvage some portion of this evening. He offered to drive, but Annabella begged for him not to and to let Meade drive. So he sat in the back while the girls sat in the front conspiring the whole way to Alys Beach and Grace's house. "Wish me luck," Annabella said as she jumped out of the car.

"I'll be back to get you at eleven," Ryder said, knowing Annabella had forgotten he was even in the backseat.

"We'll see," Annabella said. Ryder got out of the car, and Annabella looked mortified. "Dad, please. This is why I wanted Meade to bring me."

"I will be here at eleven. Be right here on the front

porch at that exact moment."

She rolled her eyes and headed inside. Ryder got in the front seat, and they waited for the door to open. Once Annabella was safely inside, Meade took off.

"I'm sorry tonight hasn't turned out like we'd hoped," he said.

"Are you kidding? I got amazing tacos and chocolate chip cookies. I'm all set."

He wanted to comment on how good she was with Annabella, but he was scared to upset the apple cart. Maybe not saying anything was a better way to go.

"Can I interest you in a decent bottle of wine? I've got two and a half hours before I need to pick her up. I could probably do one glass, but you can have as much as you want. I could take you home when I go to pick her up."

She slid him a quick look then put her gaze back on the road. "Are you trying to plow me with alcohol for any particular reason, Ryder?"

God, she really was the perfect woman. Great with her kid, baked cookies, and then moved right back into sexual innuendo mode.

When they pulled up in the driveway, she looked over at him. "I should go."

"You really should stay, just until eleven when I've got to go pick her up."

She let her head fall back onto the headrest, considering him.

"At least come inside and tell me what your magic touch is with Annabella."

"I don't have any magic touch."

"The hell you don't. You should've seen the change in her from when I called you to when you walked in the door. You brought her back to life."

"I'm just a shiny new toy. This is the honeymoon between her and me."

"She's never connected with someone I've dated like

65

this."

"Yeah, but remember, I was her friend first."

"True," he said, realizing that for the first time.

"Trust me, I'll do something to screw it up, then she'll hate me and never want to see me again. Let's just see how long it takes."

"Well, she's not home right now. Come inside and have that glass of wine. I've got a fantastic ocean view."

"I got a glimpse of it earlier. I think marine biologists make more than you're letting on."

"This house is a perk of the job."

"You're living here rent-free?"

"The house belongs to the private company I work for. They're putting me up here through the entirety of the job."

"I'm starting to think you're an important marine biologist. Someone who means a lot to certain people, with special skills and all of that."

He shrugged. "It's possible. But I'm thinking you mean a lot to certain people as well."

She just pursed her lips and set her elbow on the door frame.

"One glass?" he asked.

She rolled her eyes and opened the door, sending his heart on a catapult to the sky.

He showed her to the deck and she seated herself on the rocking love seat. That had to be a signal from her. She could've sat in one of the chairs.

He went inside and got the bottle of wine and a couple of glasses, bringing it all outside.

He set the glasses down and took the bottle. "My favorite part about this particular bottle..." He unscrewed the lid.

"Screw off wine bottles are the way to go. They're kind of hard to find in a decent wine though. Kudos to you."

"I do like this one." He poured both glasses and then sat down next to her, handing her one.

They clinked glasses.

"Cheers." She took a drink and then nodded. "Nice."

"I think you owe me a story."

She rolled her eyes, tucking her hand beneath her thigh. "You don't want to hear about that. You're entirely too normal for my mess."

"Maybe I'm not as boring as you think I am."

"I never said you were boring."

"I'll take that as a compliment. Tell me about the last guy."

"He's ancient history. He's not relevant now."

"Neither is Elise, but I told you about her...at your request, by the way."

"Understood. His name was Max. I met him at a bar. Brought him home for the night and he never left. At least not for a few months."

He cringed, imagining why the guy never left. They were probably having constant sex. Not that he'd ever gotten to experience something like that. But he'd seen movies and heard stories about people who stayed in bed for days or weekends at a time, only pulling themselves away for work and food.

"How did it end?"

"With him in bed with another woman."

"In your bed?"

She nodded, staring out at the sea. "I know this sounds like such a cliché, but I felt so violated. Those were my sheets that I had just washed. It sounds ridiculous, but that was the thing I was the most pissed about. This woman had tainted my clean sheets."

"Were you concerned at all about STIs," he asked, unable to help himself. It was the scientist in him.

"I got tested for everything, but for the record, I never have unprotected sex." She slid him a warning glance.

67

He tossed up his free hand. "No argument here."

She studied him, letting a little smile slip through, giving him sweet hope for the evening.

"Did you kick him out or did he go willingly?"

"I left. I came here, actually. My sister was here on vacation at the time, and she had tried to get me to come. So, I packed a suitcase and flew down here. I paid a ridiculous amount for a plane ticket at the last minute, but it was worth it just to get away from him." She huffed a laugh. "I also completely cock-blocked my sister without knowing I was doing it. She had spent the week with this guy and was deeply in love with him. I thought it was just some guy. Turns out it was the guy she married."

"That's pretty cool if it turned out good in the end."

"It was totally uncool. I ruined their last night together. But it worked out. He moved to Indy just for her."

"But then they both came back down here eventually," he said.

"Wouldn't you rather be here than in Indy?"

He shrugged his agreement. "Have you dated anyone since?"

She gauged him. "Define dated."

Ryder had never been a jealous guy. The relationships he had been in had been secure and predictable. It was completely ludicrous that he was finding himself jealous of guys who were in Meade's past. And she wasn't even his…yet.

"I know you're not judging me," she said with a raised eyebrow.

"No, not at all."

"Then what's that look on your face?"

He was caught and he knew it. He hated that he wore his emotions on his sleeve like that. "Maybe I'm a little jealous."

She considered this. "Of me or of the fact that I have one-night stands?"

He thought about that for a minute. "Maybe a little of both."

"You know you can have your own one-night stand anytime you want."

"I can?" he asked with raised eyebrows.

She smiled. "Maybe not any time."

"Seriously, I don't like the idea of other guys touching you."

"That's pretty possessive for a guy who has only known me a few days."

"I've known you longer than that. I met you a couple of months ago. You wanted nothing to do with me. You thought I was a stalker, didn't you?"

"I didn't know. I did think you were pretty cute."

"This is an interesting turn of events. I thought you looked like you'd rather be wrestling a grizzly bear."

"I just didn't like the kind of guy you appeared to be."

"What kind of guy was that?"

"Responsible, decent job, looking for a relationship."

He picked at a nick in the armrest. "I have been that guy. And maybe I was that guy a little bit, but you intrigued me. It was your reading selections at the library. I thought it gave me an opening to talk to you. Otherwise, I never would've gone up to you."

"Why?"

"Because I would've thought you were out of my league."

"The reading material put me in your league?"

"It gave me something to talk about that we had in common. But you don't seem to want to talk about any of that stuff."

"My reading's for me."

"It's okay to talk about books and documentaries. There's no law against it."

"No, but if I start talking with you about intelligent things, we're going to form a relationship of some sort. I

69

don't want that."

"Aren't we in a relationship right now? Isn't a friendship a relationship?"

"Is that what we are, Ryder, friends?"

There she went again with his name. He loved the way it rolled off her tongue with confident intention.

"I would call you a friend. I'd also like to call you a friend with benefits."

She just smiled and shook her head.

He poked her in the leg. "Come on, that kiss last night was pretty damn good. Don't you want to do that again?"

"You've got to go pick up your daughter."

He looked down at his phone. "Not for a while."

"You're never gonna learn. I'm not going to have sex with you because of convenient timing."

"I'm not talking about sex. I'm talking about another kiss."

"Kisses lead places."

"We could see where this kiss takes us." He ran his knuckles down the outside of her thigh.

She watched his hand move. "If I let you have one kiss, how do I know you'll leave it at that?"

"How do you know you'll want me to?"

She stared into his eyes, and he knew he had a green light. He moved in, pressing his lips against hers, keeping the moment innocent for a minute until he nudged her mouth open, and all bets were off. He'd never had chemistry like this with a woman. Just the kiss alone made him hard. He hoped she didn't notice, but he couldn't help himself. Everything about her was sensual. He hadn't understood his own sexuality until now. He'd only known comfortable, polite sex with his previous partners. He'd had plenty of foreplay and oral pleasures, but no one had made his heart pump the way Meade did just with a look, much less her tongue in his mouth. He felt like he was coming alive for the first time in his life.

She pulled away with a smile. "I think you're a big fat liar."

"What makes you say that?" He rested his hand on her thigh, moving his thumb up and down.

"You kiss like a guy who's had a lot of one-night stands."

"I've had girlfriends."

"Guys don't kiss their girlfriends like that."

"Maybe you bring out a different side of me. Maybe we should explore that side." He ran his hand around the outside of her thigh and down her leg.

"We don't have enough time to explore. I'm not having a quickie with you."

His phone buzzed and he reached over and picked it up.

Grace asked if I could spend the night.

His heart took a leap off of a tire swing. He showed Meade his phone. She rolled her eyes with a lazy smile.

"You truly are a lucky man, aren't you?"

He waggled his eyebrows.

She kicked off her flip flops then stood and walked down the steps of the deck onto the beach. "Maybe I should have become a marine biologist. You can't beat living on the beach."

He texted Grace back with the okay, and then followed Meade. He wasn't giving up. If she didn't want to be there, she wouldn't be. She had a car sitting right out front. She just wanted to be chased a little. And he certainly didn't mind doing the chasing.

"There's still time to do that or anything else you want to do."

"Or I could do nothing at all."

"Is that what you want?" he asked, pinching her hip quickly as he stepped around her.

"For the moment. This vibe is working for me."

He glanced around. The beach was dark except for

lights coming from the houses a hundred yards away. "It's working for me too."

"What are the chances of me getting you to skinny-dip in the ocean?" she asked.

If any of his neighbors could see him from this far away in the pitch-black dark, he'd be run out of town. But he'd be damned if he was going to step away from her dare. "I'm up for it if you are."

She meandered toward him, holding his eye contact with that gaze that made his body tingle. She pulled his shirt right up over his head, discarding it, daring him with her blue eyes.

Playing along, he tugged her shirt over her head, and she didn't argue. She stood there before him in a hot pink bra and jean shorts, looking like something out of his wet dreams.

He pulled her toward him by the waistband of her shorts, unbuttoning them and lowering the zipper. They slid to her feet, leaving her with nothing but a hot pink pair of panties between them.

She tugged his button loose, unzipping his pants as she looked down at them. She was about to see just how much he liked her. She set her hands on his waist, moving them around to his ass cheeks, and then pressing him against her. "When did this happen?"

"When you kissed me."

She glanced at the houses then met his gaze. "How close are you with your neighbors?"

"The one to my left is a rental. The one to my right are snowbirds. I don't think they're home right now."

She took his hand and walked into the water, and he followed her into the dark sea and all of its danger. When they were waist deep, she turned toward him, running her fingers through his hair.

"The scariest thing out here isn't even the sharks," he said.

"Oh yeah?" She ran her hand down his back. "What is it?"

"The way you make me feel." He closed his eyes as she ran her hand under the waistband of his boxers and right down the middle of his ass. Leave it to her to open with a risqué move. He hiked her up onto him and pulled her in for an urgent kiss as he grew even harder against her.

"I didn't think you'd really skinny dip with me," she said.

"You'll find I'm not as predictable as you think."

"Take me to your bed," she said, and he let her down. The two of them splashed their way to the shore and grabbed their clothes before heading into his house.

He could not get there fast enough.

Chapter Nine

Ryder closed the sliding glass door, turned, and swept Meade off her feet like a bride. A schoolgirl giggle escaped as she wrapped her arms around his neck, letting him take her to his bed. They didn't bother pulling the comforter back. He just dropped her on top and climbed over her.

Knowing she would not be able to control herself tonight, she had worn the front clasp bra, which he undid with ease. He took her nipple into his mouth, massaging the other breast, then kissed her mouth urgently as he pressed himself against her, their cold underwear still between them.

He stood and pulled his boxers to the floor, revealing his rock-hard cock. Damn that looked good. For a nerd, he was hung like a jock.

She slid out of her bra and underwear, and he went to the nightstand. "Before you do that..." she said, moving to the edge of the bed and taking him into her mouth. She loved the idea of making him crazy with want, and by the way he cupped her head, she knew he was desperately wanting.

No man had ever made her feel so desired. Meade was in charge of her own sexuality and had been since that day of her sixteenth birthday, but she understood now that Ryder's attention to her was something that made her feel authentically sexual. If she'd been smart, she'd have led him on a little longer. But she couldn't deny him another moment. She'd never wanted a man this badly.

He tugged himself away from her. "That feels too good."

"Then grab a condom," she said, scooting back on the bed. He did as he was told, readying himself before sliding his hand between them and plunging a finger inside of her, making her arch her back with want. She knew he was just checking to see if she was wet enough, and she definitely was. It didn't take long to get ready for him.

He pulled away and then entered her with a push. She pressed her palms against the headboard as he moved inside of her, their bodies joined in perfect harmony as he pumped in and out, bringing them into a rhythm.

"Oh, fuck. I'm not gonna last," he said.

"Hang on," she said to him, wrapping her hands around his shoulders and pulling him to her. She wanted to come with him.

"Okay," he said, slowing down, getting himself together. Every push inside of her made her one step closer to sweet release. She was never able to come this fast. But they had been in an intense game, and by the time she lay down on his bed, she was halfway there.

She let him know through her moans and groans that she was right there, and he pushed harder and faster, the two of them letting go in a noisy release. She was so thankful no one was home, not only in this house, but at least in one house next-door. She didn't know what to say for the renters.

He collapsed on top of her, breathing into her neck. He gave it a nibble and then pulled away, smiling at her. "That was fucking unbelievable." He didn't cuss often, but when he did, it made her smile. He narrowed his gaze at her. "So did you...?"

"What, I wasn't loud enough for you?"

"No, you were perfectly expressive. It's just that sometimes women don't do that so easily."

She lifted an eyebrow. "Are you calling me easy, Ryder?" She loved how she made him grin.

"No, I mean...never mind."

"You mean through intercourse, right?"

"Yeah," he said, running his hand over her stomach, which made her a little self-conscious. She had to start eating better.

"That's never been a problem for me."

"Great," he said.

"What, you're relieved that you didn't have to go down on me for twenty minutes?"

His cheeks went pink, making her belly sizzle. "No, I would very much like to do that." He ran his hand up her torso and between her breasts, sliding his thumb over her nipple.

It was amazing what his touch did to her. This was usually the moment she darted out of bed, but she was having trouble pulling herself away. The faint sound of her text ringtone in the next room got her attention.

He kissed her neck. "Do you need to get that?"

It could be anyone, or some random group text. A small part of her was worried it was Maya, upset because she just lost another baby. What were the chances of that being the case at this exact moment? "I'm good," she said, settling into his kisses.

Just as she was putting the text out of her mind, the tone went off again, giving her pause.

"Are you sure you don't need to get it?" he asked, moving down her body.

"I'm sure," she breathed.

Just as he was about to center himself in front of her, the text went off again.

He dropped his head onto her inner thigh, closing his eyes. "I'll go get it for you."

She ran her fingers through his hair. "Thank you. Just in case it's my sister."

"No problem," he said, taking a nibble at her thigh and rolling off of her.

He came back, holding his phone in one hand and hers in the other. He frowned at the screen of her phone, which made her extremely uncomfortable.

"Not trying to be nosy, but it's my daughter."

"Is it a group text with me and you?"

He checked his phone. "No." He handed Meade her phone and she read the texts.

Can you please come and get me?

And don't tell my dad.

Please?

Meade looked up at Ryder.

"I'm sorry," he said. "I don't know why she's texting you and not me." He thumbed into his phone. "I'm finding out what's going on now."

The swoosh of a text being sent sounded, and they waited without words for a return text to come through. But Meade's phone was the only one that buzzed.

Make up something for my dad. I'll tell him I got a ride home.

Ryder looked at her expectantly, and she passed him her phone like she had been caught with a note in class. He ran his hand through his hair, his face going blood red.

This was way more than Meade had bargained for. She felt bad for Annabella because not even knowing what was going on with her, Meade could relate. She'd been caught a time or two in high school in a bad situation and just needed out. She would've loved to have had somebody like herself now to come and rescue her without demanding all the gory details. But Annabella's very involved, visibly angry father was standing in front of Meade. Annabella had been busted and didn't even know it. And as much as Meade wanted to help, she was completely out of her depth.

She related way more with Annabella than she did with Ryder. Meade had never been a parent, but she had been a fifteen-year-old girl in trouble.

Meade slid off of the bed and tiptoed past Ryder, who barely even noticed she was on the move. Once she was in the living room and into her shorts and T-shirt, Ryder walked in, still naked. "I'm so sorry," he said.

"No, it's fine. I'm just gonna get out of here." She looked up at him. "Unless you need me to…"

"No, of course not. I'm gonna go get her."

"Cool," Meade said, and then looked around a little displaced, knowing she was forgetting something. It was her bra and underwear. They were in the other room, but screw them. "Okay, good luck." She grabbed her purse and bolted.

Chapter Ten

Ryder tried very hard not to be angry with his daughter as he drove toward the Alys Beach mansion. Or at least he needed to be angry with her for the right reasons. Or maybe he didn't need to be mad at all. There was a reason she had attempted to enlist Meade's help, and it couldn't be good. But no matter what had happened, he couldn't help the fury and hurt that built up inside of him.

She had planned to lie to him. How many times had she lied before? He felt like he didn't know his own daughter, which seemed impossible. It'd been just the two of them since his mother had died when Annabella was three. But now he felt like there was a Grand Canyon-sized crater between them.

He couldn't even think right now about the position Meade had been put in and what that could do to their budding relationship. Meade was like a butterfly that has landed on his finger. He was hoping she would stay there a long time but knew she could fly away at any moment. This was just the kind of thing to nudge her off.

When he had texted his daughter to let her know to stop texting Meade and that he was on his way, she had asked if he could meet her down the street from the house. He found her pacing on the side of the road near a construction site, which was jarring to him. No one was around. The possibilities of what could've happened to her invaded his brain and he batted them off like gnats, or more like killer wasps.

Annabella got in the car, buckled up, and then started scrolling through her phone like they were on the way to the grocery store.

"Are you okay?" he asked.

"Yes, I told you that in the text earlier."

"I don't like that you refused to take my phone call."

"I couldn't. I was in a weird situation. I needed to text. Will you please just drive?"

He reluctantly put the car in gear and they drove toward home. He had so many things he wanted to ask her. What had happened? Why had she tried to get Meade to lie to him? Was she really okay? Did they need to go to a hospital? She looked perfectly fine sitting there, but what had really happened? His stomach rolled at the possibilities.

But instead of asking any of that, he just drove, clutching the wheel until they pulled into the driveway. Once they stopped and she tried to get out, he said, "Wait. I just need to know that you're okay. Did anything happen?"

She narrowed her gaze on him. "You told me once that if I ever got into a situation I didn't want to be in that all I needed to do was call you to come get me and you would with no questions asked."

Dammit was he regretting having made that statement. Parents make those kinds of offers just to get their kids home safely. They don't think about how to handle it if their kid actually takes them up on it.

He stared at her for a moment, knowing he was stuck. "Okay."

They went inside and Annabella headed directly to her bedroom, shutting the door behind her. He collapsed on the living room couch, staring at the wall. What if she had been raped? What if they needed to be in a hospital right now having her examined and treated with post-rape medications? What if there was a little teenage prick out there on the loose?

He kept looking over at her bedroom wanting desperately to knock on the door. It wasn't like she was going to give him any information anyway. These were the moments he desperately needed a mother for her. Someone who could go in there and help her through this.

He had no one to call. He didn't have any brothers or sisters who had kids. His mother and father were both deceased. He wasn't necessarily close enough with anybody at work to drop this kind of bomb on them. He'd done a very poor job forging friendships over the past year. Work and Annabella had been his life. He had friends he kept up with from college, but no one he felt comfortable enough calling right now. A few of them had kids, but they were little kids. Nobody he knew had teenagers. Everyone else had used condoms like smart people.

But there was one person who could help him through this. Meade could find out what happened. He chewed on his thumbnail. He didn't want to burden her with this, but he was desperate. His daughter had been through something. He just needed to know she was okay. And if she wasn't, he needed to help her through whatever she had gone through, or at the very least be aware of it.

There were steps to be taken after a sexual assault. Time was ticking into a maddeningly frustrating void. This could possibly end any chance of moving forward with Meade, but first and foremost, he was a father. And his daughter needed help. He would do anything, lose anything, to get her what she needed.

He texted Meade.

I've got her home. Just wanted to let you know and apologize again.

Thanks for letting me know. I'm glad she's safe now.

He hoped Meade would ask more questions, but that wasn't her style. She wasn't nosy.

I'm a little worried. She's home but she's not talking. I hope nothing serious happened.

A few minutes went by, and then his phone rang. It was Meade. A wash of hope poured over him as he answered the call.

"If you want me to talk to her, you just have to ask, Ryder."

He closed his eyes, emotion pouring over him. "I'm desperate, Meade. I need your help."

"I'll be over in a few." The phone disconnected and he let it drop down to his lap, covering his eyes, holding back the emotion trying to overtake him.

Chapter Eleven

Meade couldn't believe it wasn't midnight yet. In the course of a few hours, she had bonded with a teenage girl, skinny dipped in the ocean, had sex with a hot nerd, and was on her way back to his house to play therapist to his daughter. Her life was atypical, but even this was a lot for her.

If she hadn't felt the desperation in his text and the relief in his voice, she would be more irritated about what she was being asked to do. But he was a desperate father. Even though she had never been a parent, she could understand that.

Ryder had the front door opened before she even approached it. He must've been watching for her out the window.

"Thank you so much for coming," he said in a hushed voice.

"It's fine. I get it."

"She's locked in her bedroom."

"Why don't you go to your bedroom and shut the

door."

He looked at her with wide eyes.

"Ryder, if anything serious has happened I'm going to tell you. But if you want me to do this, you need to give us some privacy."

It felt weird to be ordering him around when it was his daughter at play here. But Meade was not at all comfortable talking to Annabella and getting her to open up to her with him listening in at the door. Not that he would do that, but he would be straining to hear.

He gave a reluctant nod and went to his room. Meade waited for the door to shut before she knocked on Annabella's door.

"It's Meade. Will you let me in?"

A moment later, the door opened and Annabella wiped her eyes. "What are you doing here?"

"I just wanted to see what was up. And I wanted to apologize about not responding to you."

She motioned Meade inside, looking into the living room before shutting the door behind them. "Why didn't you respond?" she asked, giving Meade a pouty look.

"Your dad intercepted my phone. He saw your messages before I did."

She rolled her eyes and collapsed onto her bed. "I should've known. You didn't seem like the type who would tattle."

That sentence made Meade uncomfortable because the whole purpose of her being there was to report to Ryder. Nothing about the situation was comfortable for her and she was starting to resent being put in this position. There were hundreds of easy guys in this area. Why did Meade have to choose a difficult one for tonight's fun?

"Do you want to tell me what happened tonight?"

"I don't want to talk about it."

"I get it. Sometimes we just want to be home. Been there. Do you want to watch a movie on your phone?"

Meade knew that pushing was not the right way to get the information. "We didn't finish the other movie."

"I don't have a DVD player back here."

"We'll stream it," Meade said, and pulled up the app on her phone, purchasing the movie for streaming. "Want to start from the beginning or do you wanna pick up where we left off?"

"Pick up where we left off."

"Cool," Meade said and found her way to that point. They sat together watching the movie with not nearly as many laughs as they had before. After about twenty minutes, Annabella said, "I'm inexperienced."

Meade turned the volume down. "I would hope so. You're only fifteen."

"What were you like at fifteen?"

Meade chuckled. "I'd never even kissed a boy."

"Really?"

"Yeah."

"When did you have sex for the first time?"

Meade pursed her lips at her. "I wasn't fifteen."

Annabella gave her a no bullshit look. "Sixteen?"

"More like nineteen."

"Really?"

"Yeah. I was a total chickenshit. I talked a big game, but when it would come down to it, I wasn't ready. It was freaking scary."

Annabella's eyes went wide. "Yeah, it is. Why is that?"

"You don't want to make a wrong decision or let some asshole take your heart. And that's not even factoring in all the STIs that are out there. And pregnancy. Sex is scary as shit."

Annabella wiggled in her place on the bed, crossing her arms over her stomach.

"Did some little asshole try to get you to do something you didn't want to do tonight?"

"No. Well, kind of. It was sort of a group thing. Like a spin the bottle kind of game, I guess, except they weren't kissing." She gave Meade a significant look, and she used her creativity to fill in the blanks.

"Ah. So were other girls actually following through, or was it all just kind of a joke?"

"Grace followed through."

That did not surprise Meade in the least. "In front of everyone?"

"No, they went in the closet."

"Oh, so there's no proof that she actually followed through with it."

"I mean, no proof, but I'm sure she did. She has no qualms about anything, ever."

"What about the other girls who were there?"

"There was just one other girl there and the guy she's been seeing was there, so they did it."

"In the closet, right?"

"Yeah."

"Then we don't know that they really did."

"Well, no, not technically, but it was pretty obvious the way they both looked guilty when they came out."

"Hmm. So, to you, it's feeling like everyone in the world who's your age is doing this and you're the last one to the party, I'm guessing."

Annabella slid Meade a look and then gazed down at her lap nodding.

"First of all, I'd bet a hundred dollars nobody went down on anybody in that closet."

Annabella giggled with Meade's turn of phrase, confirming that was what was happening, allegedly.

"And secondly, even if that is what was going on, that doesn't have to be your path. If you're not ready for that, you don't need to let these asshole kids talk you into it. You wait as long as you want to wait. You're in control of your body, not Grace or some needle-dick kid."

Annabella's sweet face contorted into a ball of stress, and Meade hoped she didn't step over a line, but she probably did. She was damn sure not qualified for this.

"So did you end up in that closet?" Meade asked, treading lightly.

Annabella fiddled with her phone, finally giving a nod.

Meade nodded in return as if this was typical. She didn't want Annabella to feel any worse than she already did. "Are you okay?"

"I didn't go through with it. But I probably should have."

"No, you shouldn't have. Not if you didn't want to."

"But the alternative is more than I can handle. I got up to leave but they had the door barricaded. I started banging on it and they were all laughing, even the guy in the closet with me. He just gave me this look like I was this total newb."

Meade wished she could get a hold of these little asshole kids without consequences. "What happened when they finally opened the door?"

"I just walked outside. Nobody even followed me. Now I've got to face them all at school. They're going to make fun of me in the hallway and at lunch. I'm going to be that kid everybody laughs at. I can't believe that's going to be me."

Meade let out a sigh, wishing she could solve this girl's high school drama. God knows Meade had had enough of her own. "If it happens it happens."

"How would you handle it?"

"Well, when I was your age, I probably would've hidden in the bathroom. But now that I'm in my thirties, I have a little more perspective. I'd probably just stick up my middle finger and move on." She thought about it a minute. "Or there is another route."

"What's that?"

"I'm not sure if this is something I should be saying to

you."

Annabella grabbed her arm. "Please, Meade, I'm desperate. I'm so worried about this. You have no idea."

"You could annihilate this guy in front of people. Like make fun of the size of his dick or something."

Annabella's eyes went wide. "But I didn't even see it. He started unzipping and that's when I freaked out."

"They don't know you didn't see it. It's your word against his. These kids just want somebody to make fun of. Just as long as it's not them, that's all that matters. If this guy was no help to you, then he's worthless and fair game."

"What would you say exactly?"

Meade thought about it a second. "All right. Let's say they're giving you a hard time, calling you a newb or whatever. And he's standing right there playing along. You could say something like, 'I'm gonna need a dick bigger than my pinky if I'm gonna have a good time.'"

Annabella's hand flew to her mouth as she giggled. "I can't say that."

"You asked what I would say. It might not be the right thing for you to say."

Annabella dropped her shoulders. "I wish you could come to school with me."

"No thanks. I'm thrilled to be done with all of that."

"But you love reading so much."

"On my own terms. What I want to read. I don't like somebody else telling me what I need to read or study."

"Me either."

Meade nudged her. "Yeah, but I think Florida state law says you've got to."

"And the law of my dad, which is even harsher."

Meade chuckled. "For sure." She considered Annabella. "Any chance you could tell your dad you're okay?"

"I already said that."

"Yeah, but he's worried you're not telling him the truth."

"He's calling me a liar?"

"Didn't you ask me to lie for you tonight?"

Annabella looked contrite. "All right. You're not gonna tell him anything I said, are you?"

Meade's stomach sizzled. "No. I won't."

Annabella's face relaxed with relief. "Thank you. I just needed someone to talk this through with."

"We all need someone sometimes."

Annabella nodded, looking down at her phone.

"Are you getting tired?" Meade asked.

"I don't know how I'm gonna go to sleep tonight. I'm just going to be sitting here worried about it."

"Give me your phone," Meade said, and then pulled up an album. "Listen to this from beginning to end. Really listen to all the lyrics and the music and let this take you to sleep tonight. It's my go to."

"Cool," Annabella said and then gave Meade a smile.

Meade stood up. "I'm gonna head home. Report back to me on that album tomorrow. I want to know your thoughts."

"Will do."

"Don't worry about this. Worry is such a useless action."

Annabella nodded. "Yeah. Definitely."

Meade wiggled her fingers in a wave and then closed the door behind her as she left. She was already at her car when the front door opened and Ryder came hustling out. Meade shook her head at him. "Obvious at all?"

"I just need to know if she's okay."

"She's okay."

"Are you sure? Is there anything I need to do or..."

"There's nothing you need to do. Just let her get some sleep."

He let out a hard breath. "I don't know what I

would've done without you tonight."

Meade winced. She couldn't be someone's ride or die. "I'll see you later, okay?" Meade got in the car, backing out without giving him a second look.

Chapter Twelve

As Ryder mined data on his computer screen, he found that the podcast he usually listened to was not connecting with him. He couldn't get his mind off of the women in his life. He split his time thinking about the things he and Meade had done in his bed Saturday night and worrying about his daughter, though the worry was just residual at this point, like shrapnel from a bomb.

He didn't know what he would've done without Meade. Whether she liked or knew it, she cared about his daughter. It was all over her face. He read her expression when she showed up at the door that night. She was worried. Her worry had made him feel less alone in that particular parenting crisis.

But when she had come out of Annabella's room, she was the cool, laid-back person he knew her to be. She had completely settled his nerves. It seemed like he had help for the first time since his mother died.

But Meade had been cool ever since. She wasn't ghosting him, but she wasn't engaging with his texts either. Saturday night had been intense, and he needed to give her space. He understood that. It was just difficult, because he wanted to see her again. He wanted to talk to her. He wanted to do lots of other things with her and to her.

His phone buzzed, grabbing his attention. It was the school calling. He picked up the phone. "Hello?"

"Yes, Mr. Lambert?"

"Speaking."

"This is Assistant Vice Principal, Doctor Parnell calling."

Ryder sat up straight. "Yes?"

"I was wondering if you had a moment to talk."

"Of course."

"I'd prefer you come down to the school."

"Is everything okay?"

"We just have some concerns we'd like to discuss and these things are sometimes easier to do in person."

"Okay," Ryder said, looking around, a little displaced. He'd never been called to the principal's office. He didn't have any idea what kinds of concerns the man was talking about, but his concerns about Annabella's safety were now back in play. "I'm available now."

"I've got an opening at two-thirty. Can you make it then?"

"Certainly," Ryder said. He finished the conversation and then hung up the phone wondering how he was going to make it through the next hour and a half without letting his mind wander to dark places. His logical side told him there was nothing to worry about until he knew exactly what the problem was. But he was human, and worrying was just part of being a parent.

Waiting in the reception area of the principal's office with the school secretary busying herself made him feel about twelve. It also made him feel like demanding that she open the door and let him into that man's office to see exactly what was going on.

After what seemed like an eternity, the door opened and a kid walked out of the office, leaving a man, slight in build and stature but radiating authority, standing in front of him, sighing as if cleaning his pallet for the next taste.

When the man made eye contact with him, Ryder stood, dwarfing the man by a good eight to ten inches. "Mister Lambert?" the man asked.

"Yes," Ryder said.

"I'm Assistant Principal Parnell. Please, come have a seat." Ryder followed the man into his office and sat down. "Thank you for coming in on such short notice. Everything's fine with Annabella, but I would like to discuss some unusual behavior of hers."

"Okay," Ryder said, his mind whirling with possibilities, none of them good.

"If this were another kid, I would've taken disciplinary action and moved on. But we witnessed some behavior today that seemed a bit out of line for Annabella. I've been around teenagers a long time, so there's little that shocks me. But when I see one of the more promising students falling down an askew path, I like to get the parents involved as soon as possible."

"What kind of path?" Ryder asked, not sure whether to be grateful or pissed off.

The man let out a sigh and then looked Ryder in the eye. "Typically, the kids do this kind of thing on social media and the school doesn't really have any involvement. But in Annabella's case, with her access to the resources of the yearbook committee, she was able to print off this picture and post it in all the girls' bathrooms. Since the incident happened on school property, we have to have a bit more involvement."

The assistant principal handed Ryder a piece of paper

with a picture of a teenage boy on it with the caption *I have limp dick and can't find a clit with GPS.*

Ryder's brain could not compute what was happening. He passed the picture back to the man. "I find it hard to believe Annabella had anything to do with this."

"She admitted to it."

Ryder felt his resolve crumble. He pinched the bridge of his nose. "Okay."

"I know this is a shock. This is why I've asked you to come here. It doesn't line up with what we have gotten to know of her personality over the past year. Often times these types of things are picked up from their friends or someone they've seen online."

"I monitor her internet usage," Ryder said, realizing how naïve the statement was the second it came out of his mouth.

"I imagine you do. I know you are Annabella's primary parent. Father to father, I know conversations with teenage daughters can be difficult. My daughter is sixteen. It's been...a challenge. My wife has handled all the difficult conversations. Does Annabella have anyone she can confide in? A mentor or an aunt?"

Ryder thought about Meade and then erased the idea out of his mind. He never thought he would be the father looking into the pitying eyes of a principal, but here he was. He stood. "I will handle this. I assume she's being punished here at school?"

"She'll need to come to detention this afternoon and tomorrow afternoon where she will be required to write an essay explaining what she did wrong and how she will change her behavior in the future."

Ryder nodded. "Good."

"Additionally, and this isn't necessarily punishment, but a group from the Philanthropy Club will be taking a bus on Saturday to Pensacola to paint a school. There are some good kids in this group. It may be good for

Annabella to be around them and do some manual labor...see a different side of high school life."

"She'll be there. And this will not happen in the future. I can guarantee that."

The principal gave him a nod with a look on his face that said he was not nearly as certain about that statement as Ryder was.

As Ryder sat in the parking lot waiting for Annabella to come out after detention, he gave himself a pep talk about staying levelheaded, but the second the car door opened, he lost any sense of sanity. "What were you thinking?" She slammed the car door shut and pulled out her phone. He snatched it away from her. "Annabella, you have screwed up in a major way. I need to know why you would do something like this."

"I just did, okay?"

"No, not okay."

"The guy's an asshole."

"Since when do you speak that way?"

She rolled her eyes. "Please. You can't think that people my age don't cuss."

He kneaded his knuckle into his forehead, realizing that cussing was the least of his problems. "What led you here?" She just looked at him blankly. "Why did you do this to this boy?"

"He is not some innocent boy. He is a total jerk. Just leave it at that, okay?"

"Not okay at all." They sat in a stalemate until Ryder finally said, "Did this have something to do with what happened Saturday night?"

When she crossed her arms over her chest and stared out the window, he knew he was right.

"Did this kid do something to you?" he said, trying not to grit his teeth.

She just craned her neck farther away from him.

"I need to know if something happened to you. You don't have to tell me specifics, but I need to know."

"I'm fine. I told you I'm fine."

"Were you…" He cleared the frog in his throat. "Were you assaulted in some way?"

Her face scrunched up. "No. But this guy did something to embarrass me, so I embarrassed him back. We're even now."

"Since when do we get even?"

"Since now. You should have perspective on this anyway now that you're like a million years old or something."

"Perspective? What kind of perspective?"

"Maybe when you were my age you would've just let it go. But I'm not that person anymore. I'm going to stand up for myself, even if it means getting in trouble."

He didn't know how to respond to that. He couldn't really argue it. "I don't know what this is about, but I know what you did is wrong. Do you at least understand that?"

She rolled her eyes. "Yes, Dad. I just spent an hour writing an essay on it."

"I want to read it."

"You can't. I turned it in."

"Then write me a new one."

"You're not serious?"

"I'm dead serious. You can rewrite the essay you wrote earlier or write me a new one. But I need to know that you are contrite about this and understand why you can't do things like what you did today."

"Fine. Is that It?"

"No," Ryder said, feeling his way here. He'd never had to punish her like this before. Was writing an essay enough? He didn't have any clue. He'd already stolen the principal's punishment. "You're grounded."

"For how long?"

"Two weeks," he said, pulling an arbitrary time period out of his ass.

"Dad," she said like he was the biggest idiot on the planet.

"Do you want three?"

She turned her head away from him and he put the car in gear.

"And you're painting a school on Saturday with the Philanthropy Club."

"They're total geeks."

Meade talked about how she didn't want to be a parent...didn't feel qualified. What the hell qualified him? And what had he done to initiate this left turn?

He wanted to call Meade and tell her all about it...get her opinion on his punishment. Had he been too harsh? Too lenient?

He never wanted the opinions of the women he was dating. In fact, he kept his relationship with Annabella very private from those women because of the way she never took to any of them. But everything was different with Meade, from the way she interacted with his daughter to the way she infected his brain and his heart. He was afraid she was going to be there for a very long time.

Chapter Thirteen

On Tuesday just after work, Meade's phone chirped with a text from Annabella. It was a gif of a diva fist pumping the air with the caption "Success!" underneath it. As Meade rested against the counter of the bar, she grinned as she selected her own gif in return—something sassy from one of the famous housewives.

She'd been careful with her responses since Saturday. Ryder had texted her a few times thanking her and checking in on her. Meade had kept her responses short and to-the-point. But she took a few liberties with Annabella's texts, only because Meade was human, and Annabella was a girl in need of either a mother or a best friend and had neither. Meade would ease out of both of these relationships as soon as she could, but for now, she was working through her exit strategy.

By Friday, she could tell that Ryder had gotten the hint, unfortunately. It's not like she wanted to send him away. She wanted to bring him into her bed and keep him there for a good three weeks. But this was not a situation she could be a part of. It was like a pool of quicksand. She wouldn't even know she was drowning in it until it was too late. An easy break before things got too serious was the way to go.

Heading to her car after the shift change on Friday, she was thinking about what to get for dinner when her phone beeped—a text from the billionaire. It was an article someone had written about his program for the New York Times. She got in her car and was about to head out, but she was too interested in the headline to ignore it. She tapped on it and found it was a glowing review from a writer who had spent a week on his compound in Texas. Nice play, letting someone else do the bragging for him.

Her phone dinged again while she was driving, but she ignored it. The billionaire could wait.

When she pulled up in her driveway, she checked her phone and found it was a text from Ashe, which unreasonably made her tummy flutter a little. The man was gay and taken. How ridiculous was she?

SOS!

She frowned, puzzling him out. He texted again—a gif of a desperate man on his knees with his hands clasped in prayer. She felt a favor request coming.

Desiree needs a Girl Friday. She's got an event at Gwendolen and Rob's house and the catering staff has come down with the flu. Sebastian and I are going to fill in with the food. We need all hands on deck. I'll grant you whatever wish you want.

She smiled.

Turn straight for the night?

If that damn Ethan wasn't in the picture, I'd be all yours, sweetie.

I'll take you up on it if you ever decide to break his heart.

He's got mine in his back pocket if you ever wanna try to steal it. So you're in?

You know I am. I can't resist you.

Thank God these good looks are worth something on occasion.

He texted her the address, the time to be there, and what to wear. She'd been to Gwendolen and Rob's house once before. It was actually the night she met Ryder. She'd been there as a guest that night though. Gwendolen had already hosted a show for Desiree in July. Meade couldn't imagine what this was. Although, Gwendolen had quite the social roster. Meade had heard through the grapevine that Gwendolen and Rob had met when she was cleaning his house. They had a whirlwind weekend and wound up married shortly after. Talk about going from rags to riches.

Meade went home and showered, primped, and dressed in the requisite black uniform. She hated to admit that she was relieved to have the distraction. Her heart felt a little empty this week as she tried to distance herself from Ryder. She really liked him, which was the problem, of course.

Meade was greeted at the front door by a wide-eyed Marigold. "I owe you so many drinks."

"It's not like I was meeting the Queen of England or something. What do you need me to do?"

"Sebastian, Ashe, and Blake are heading up catering."

"They're actually cooking?"

"I know it sounds insane, but Sebastian has thrown enough of these shindigs to piece together a decent menu, Blake has done some cooking for himself and Seanna that doesn't include a microwave, and Ashe loves Desiree so much that he'll fall in line and do whatever the others say...just this once. We'd love to have you behind the bar. You're the only one of this crew who has any experience."

"I can handle that."

"And balancing the federal budget according to your

sister, but tonight I'll settle for you pouring drinks. Come on in."

Meade followed Marigold inside, wishing her sister would shut the hell up about her. They walked through the living room and out the back doors onto the pool deck where the water appeared to overflow into the ocean backdrop. The bar was set up in the corner and was as big, if not bigger than, the one she worked at on the beach every day. Bo and Chase were unloading a dolly full of boxes of liquor.

"This looks like a party." Meade said by way of greeting.

Bo, her brother-in-law, looked up at her. "We got twelve bottles of vodka. Do you think that'll be enough?"

"For this and the after party."

"We got six bottles of bourbon and six of scotch," said Chase. "But I'll stay sober tonight and run out to the liquor store for anything you need as soon as you see yourself getting low. Just text me."

Marigold put her hand on Meade's forearm. "To simplify things for you, how about two or three signature drinks to help people make up their minds."

"And by people, she means women," Bo said. "Men will already have their mind made up."

"Whiskey or beer," Chase said.

"We bought these commercial coolers back here," Bo said. "We got a boatload of ice, but we still need more."

Meade took a peek inside one of the stainless-steel coolers. "This gives us a good base for the beer. Probably just need some more bags to load on top."

Bo brought her in for a hug and kissed her on the forehead like a little sister. "Maya wants to have you over for dinner this coming week."

"My dance card is full," she said, looking up at him.

Bo was all too familiar with the tension between Meade and his wife. "You know she just loves you. And so do I."

Meade rolled her eyes. "I love you both back."

"I'll grill salmon with that sesame stuff you like on it."

She gave him a smile. "It's a deal."

"We'll go grab the ice and a few more things for the guys in the kitchen. Text us with whatever else you need. When we get back, we'll help you load all the beer into the cooler."

"I'll help her," came a voice that had Meade's stomach doing a spin.

She looked up to find Ryder standing in the entryway wearing his black. His shaggy hair was all cute and ruffled, and he had his Clark Kent glasses on. She couldn't decide if she liked him better in or out of those. He was turning out to be devastatingly handsome either way.

She should've known he'd be there. She couldn't say that the thought hadn't popped into her mind. But now that she saw him, she couldn't help being thankful for that stomach flu that brought them all here.

Chase and Bo each shook Ryder's hand in that masculine guy way that men had. Ryder's shoulders lifted as he held his own with these two alphas.

They exchanged a few pleasantries and then Bo and Chase were on their way.

"I guess they called in all their reinforcements," Ryder said.

"Helps to have a lot of friends who will drop everything for you."

"I suppose you're tonight's bartender?" he asked.

"Looks that way. Have you been assigned a job yet?"

"Bartender's assistant."

Meade lifted an eyebrow. "Is that a self-appointed position?"

"More like a suggestion that Marigold agreed to."

Meade fought to hide her smile. "I'm sure they could

use you in the kitchen."

"And I'm sure I'd rather be right here," he said sliding past her, holding eye contact. He bent down and started unpacking boxes while she inhaled a deep breath, gathering her bearings. She didn't know she was in for this kind of night, but she couldn't say she was disappointed.

"Besides," he said, slicing open a box with a pocket knife, "I've got to stay out of the kitchen. Annabella's in there."

"She is?" Meade asked, wishing she had a second to go say hello.

"Yeah. She hasn't been talking to me. She's grounded. She's lucky I let her out of the house to come do this."

"What happened?" Meade asked.

He shook his head as he pulled beers out of the box. "She did something really out of character at school this week. She posted pictures of some kid all over the girls' bathrooms talking about him having limp dick. I can't believe she would do something like that. I can't believe she has those thoughts." He held up a hand. "I know I'm naïve. But that's my little girl in there."

Meade winced, thinking about her conversation with Annabella.

"I don't want to mess this up," Ryder said, holding four bottles of beer in his hands and looking at her.

"Oh, just stick all one brand together so I'll know where to grab from, generally. Did they punish her at school?" Meade asked, pulling out a bottle of bourbon and setting it on the bar.

"Detention. But worse than that, I got called to the principal's office. I managed to not get called to the principal's office my whole life until now."

Meade nodded.

He looked up at her with a smile. "How many times did you get called to the principal's office?"

"Once or twice," Meade said, her chest burning. Had she gotten Annabella in trouble? "If you don't mind, I'm just gonna go say hello to her for a minute."

"Sure," he said. "She definitely likes you better than me right now."

Meade made her way to the kitchen and spotted Annabella on a stool in the corner thumbing into her phone. "Hey," Meade said, getting her attention. Annabella's face lit up as she saw Meade. She jumped down off her stool and wrapped her arms around Meade. "Oh my gosh, I didn't know you'd be here. Can we work together?"

"I've got to tend bar."

Annabella waggled her eyebrows. "Even better."

"With your dad."

The girl's expression dropped and she hopped back onto the stool. "No thanks." She tapped into her phone again.

"What happened this week?"

Annabella put her phone down. "Oh my gosh, it was awesome. So, I'm on the yearbook committee, and we had this picture of Riley, and we made this graphic of him with a bubble that said, 'I have limp dick and can't find a clit with GPS.' We slapped them up in all the girls' bathrooms. It was amazing."

Meade scratched her head because her fifteen-year-old self wanted to squeal in laughter, but her adult self was cringing at the repercussions. "Wow," she said, trying to stay neutral.

"I know. They totally made fun of me Monday just like I knew they would, and then I thought, I don't have to take this lying down, like you said. So, I got this girl who's in yearbook with me to help me. She's sort of Goth but loves graphic design. She helped me do the whole thing."

"Did she get in trouble too?"

"Oh no. I copped to it by myself. No need to drag her

down with me. She was fantastic."

"New friend?"

"I don't know about that. She's pretty weird. But definitely a cohort of sorts."

Meade just nodded, glancing around, wondering how she got herself into this mess.

"So, you got in trouble at school and at home?"

"Yeah, but who cares. It was totally worth it."

She wasn't regretful or remorseful at all. Meade had created her own fifteen-year-old monster. "But you won't do something like that again, right?"

Annabella shrugged. "Depends on who wants to fuck with me."

Oh shit, now she had the girl throwing out the F bomb. Why was Meade allowed out of the house?

"Um...Annabella," Meade said, scratching her forehead.

Desiree swept up to the two of them, embracing them both at the same time. "You ladies are heaven sent. Thank you so much for coming to my rescue."

"No problem," Meade said.

Annabella pocketed her phone. "Put me in, coach."

"Fantastic," Desiree said. "Can I get you to circulate with the trays of food?"

Annabella shrugged. "Sure."

"You're on bar duty, right?" Desiree asked Meade.

"That's right. I'm just saying hello to Annabella."

"Of course," Desiree said. "Please stay around afterward and let's decompress together. And let me figure out a way to make this up to you."

"Not necessary," Meade said. "I'm just gonna get back to the bar."

"Thank you," Desiree said with a genuine smile. She carted Annabella off, leaving Meade trying to figure out how to reroute the train she had let off the rails.

Chapter Fourteen

The only way Ryder could describe Meade's behavior all night was unsteady. When he first arrived, she'd been her usual sexy, sly, flirtatious self. But soon after that, her demeanor changed. It was after she had gone to say hello to Annabella, which left him wondering what horrific things his daughter had said about him. Surely Meade had not fallen victim to a fifteen-year-old girl's rantings about her evil dad.

Ryder had taken it upon himself to get people's drink orders so he could interact with Meade as much as possible. He was pulling out his best material each time he approached her. He would get a smile out of her each time, but he could tell something was bothering her.

He took some glasses to the kitchen where Chase and Bo washed dishes. Every time he went in there, the two of them were flicking water in each other's faces or whipping the other one with a wet towel. Ryder had never seen two adult men act more like teenage brothers.

"Can either of you tend bar for a minute?"

"I'll do it," Chase said puffing his chest out.

Bo took the opportunity to sock him one in the stomach. "You keep your pansy ass in here. This is man's work."

"Is that why a woman's doing it right now?" Chase asked.

Bo followed Ryder through the house. "I see you've made friends with my sister-in-law. Do I need to grill you about your intentions?"

"I'd rather you grill her about hers," Ryder said.

Bo smiled. "Little hard to read, isn't she?"

"A bit."

"You know she's smarter than you and I put together, right?"

"I don't know how tough that is to accomplish," Ryder said.

Bo laughed. "That's for damn sure."

Ryder hesitated before opening the patio door. "Are you a betting man, Bo?"

"I've been known to be."

"What would you say my odds are with her?"

Bo squinted. "As long as my wife doesn't find out that Meade's interested in a guy like you with a good job and a stable life, you've got a better shot. But the second Maya finds out this is a possibility, she's going to pounce, and Meade's gonna run like hell."

"How about you tell your wife that I'm a two-timing asshole who drinks too much and just quit my job."

"That'll help."

As Ryder opened the door, Bo said, "I see you figured things out pretty quickly. I thought you seemed like a smart guy."

"I definitely don't have much figured out or I wouldn't need your help to get her alone for a second."

"Have you ever been deer hunting?" Bo asked.

"Can't say that I have."

"The key is to not make any big sudden moves." Bo lifted his eyebrows in a significant look and then stepped behind the bar. "I'm guessing you need a bathroom break."

"I'm okay," Meade said. "I snuck away a minute ago."

"Good, then you can go talk to Ryder with an empty bladder." Bo put both hands on Meade's shoulders and ushered her toward Ryder.

Meade didn't argue, but her face did color. And Ryder could feel his warming. "How about a quick walk on the beach?"

She pointed at the bar. "But I'm—"

"Covered," Bo interrupted. "Go."

She hesitated, and then followed Ryder through the pool area and down the stairs. When they got to the bottom, they found a swing and he offered her a seat, which she took. He sat next to her. "Do you want to tell me what's been going on with you tonight?"

She shrugged. "Just doing my job."

"What did Annabella say to you in the kitchen?"

She rubbed her finger against her forehead, covering her face from him. "I think I might've fucked up," she said, her hand shaking.

"Hey," he said, taking her hand and squeezing it. "Talk to me."

She shook her head. "I'm not a mother or a mother figure. I'm just a fuckup who your daughter likes, probably because she knows I'm a fuckup."

"Meade, tell me what's going on here."

She met his gaze, looking like she was feeling him out.

"Listen, she's not your daughter. She's my daughter. I called you over there the other night because I was desperate. If you said something and now you're regretful, it's on me. It's not on you. And I'm not going to be upset with you."

"Not even if I'm the reason she got in trouble this

week?"

He swallowed, determined to stay true to his word. "I doubt you did, but that's right. Even if something you said encouraged her to do that, I can't blame you."

She pulled her hand away from him, shaking her head. "I don't need to talk to her or any other teenager ever again. I'm a just a teenager myself in my head half the time. More than half the time."

"Aren't we all? Do you think I'm some kind of adult?" That made her smile, which warmed him. "Please, Meade. I'm so in the dark. I just want to know what's happening in my daughter's life. You can't imagine the desperation I feel."

She studied him. "I promised her I wouldn't say anything."

"I know you did. And I don't want you to go back on that promise. But I also need to know what's happening so I can know how to help her."

She let out a sigh. "God knows you'll do a better job than I did."

He waited her out, trying to close the sale.

"The kids she's hanging out with did something to humiliate her. She was getting them back. I didn't tell her to do that exactly, but I did suggest something that was in the ballpark of what she did."

He couldn't help himself. "What did you suggest?"

She clenched her teeth. "I just said that if they started making fun of her about the thing that happened, that she should make a joke about his dick size."

Ryder tried hard not to wince.

"I told you I completely fucked up." She started to get up and he pulled her back down.

"Meade, did one of those little monsters hurt her?"

"No. They just embarrassed her. She didn't lose anything that night."

He lowered his chin. "You know for a fact she's still a

virgin?"

Meade lifted one eyebrow. "She's a teenager. Nobody knows anything for a fact."

His shoulders lost the tension they were holding. "True."

"Look, this guy was a little dickhead. They all were, but he could've helped and he didn't. Any one of those assholes could've stood up for her. I just wanted her to know that she can take her power back. She doesn't have to walk around humiliated. She can do the humiliating if she wants."

"But that's not how we teach our kids."

"How the hell am I supposed to know that?"

He rubbed his own forehead. "I know. I'm sorry. I don't want to be a liar here. I promise I'm not mad at you."

"It doesn't feel that way," she said.

He nodded. "I know. The truth is I don't know what my advice would've been to her. Trust me when I say I was humiliated plenty in middle school. I know what that's like. And I never had a dad who advised me to stand up for myself. I was raised for the most part by my mom. She was all about peace and love. I am too, except when it comes to a fifteen-year-old fuckwad who wants to mess with my daughter. And then I just want to get a hold of him with my bare hands."

Meade lifted her eyebrows at him.

He gave her a smile. "Thank you for coming clean with me."

She pursed her lips. "Now I've just betrayed your daughter. I don't like being in this position."

"I don't like putting you in this position. There's only one position I want to put you in right now," he said, wrapping his hand around her knee.

She gave him a look with a hint of a smile. "You cannot be serious. I just told you that I have completely screwed over your parenting efforts and now you wanna have sex with me?"

"Yep," he said, leaning in to kiss her.

She pulled away with a grin. "You're out of your mind."

"Little bit." He squeezed her thigh.

"Oh my God," she said under her breath like she couldn't believe she was going to give into him. Or at least he hoped that was her intention.

"I've been thinking about you all week," he said, reaching over and kissing her neck. She had her hair up and out of the way and it was just sitting there looking good enough to lick.

"Last time I checked we were working."

"Last time I checked your brother-in-law had you covered."

"So, we're going to have sex right here in this swing somehow?"

"We almost did it in the ocean the other day."

"If you think I'm getting undressed in front of all the people who are circulating around this mansion, you're out of your mind."

"How about on that boat over there." He nodded at the dock.

"You can't be serious?"

"I'm totally serious. Nobody's down here."

"Is that Gwendolen and Rob's boat?"

"Probably."

"Do you even know them?"

"I've been out with them a time or two with Desiree."

She narrowed her gaze again. "You two are close, aren't you?"

"You're not going jealous on me now, are you?" he asked, loving it if she was.

"I'm not jealous of Desiree. I'm just trying to gauge you and see how well you know that boat."

"Well enough to know that we can christen it right

now."

"We don't even have a condom."

He pulled one out of his pocket and showed it to her. She looked around trying to wipe the smile off her face and then met his gaze. "Do you carry condoms around all the time so you can whisk random girls away to boats?"

"This is the first time I've put a condom in my pocket since high school."

"So not only did you expect to see me here tonight, but you expected to fuck me?"

"I wouldn't have grabbed the condom if not."

She covered her mouth holding back a laugh.

"What do you say? Where is your sense of adventure?"

She shook her head, looking around.

He stood up and held out his hand, not believing how big his balls had suddenly gotten. If he was caught having sex on this boat by anyone at this party, he'd have to move from South Walton to Antarctica. But it was worth every bit of that risk to get inside of her right this minute. To his delight, she stood and followed him down the beach as she glanced around.

"Nobody sees us," he said. "And if they did, they'd think we were just taking a look at the boat."

"I cannot believe I'm doing this."

"I thought you were supposed to be the wild one of the two of us," he said.

"I thought so too. I'm paranoid to step out of line after my misstep this week."

"Then I'll just have to show you the way."

They walked down the beach and onto the dock where they boarded the boat, Ryder helping her on. He peered around the deck until he found a compartment and looked inside.

"What are you doing?" she asked.

"Finding a place to ditch the condom."

"Wouldn't you typically do that after sex?"

"I like to be prepared."

She pointed at him. "Now that's the Ryder I have come to know. Pragmatic."

He reached around, hiking her up onto him, causing her to let out a little squeal. He kissed her and then sat down on the leather bench leaving her straddling him. As their kisses got more intense, she began grinding against him, getting him rock hard in seconds. He slid his hands up her shirt, grabbing handfuls of her breasts. "I love your body," he said against her mouth. "I think about it all the time."

She shut him up with more kisses, running her fingers through his hair, grinding so hard against him he was afraid he might come right there like a teenage first-timer.

She stood up off of him, letting her pants drop to the floor while he got out of his own. He started to grab for the condom, but she knelt in front of him, spreading his legs and guiding him into her mouth. He sat back, watching her. He'd never seen anything sexier in his life. He'd never known passion like this. He understood now that the women who had come before Meade had been good friends, some of whom he may have even loved. But what he felt for Meade was pure, carnal lust. It was a higher high than any drug could ever give him. And he didn't know if he would ever be able to quit her.

He nudged her away from him before he ruined the moment by giving in to the intense pleasure she gave him. "I want to taste you," he said to her.

She held his gaze while she stepped onto the couch, straddling him and lowering herself down to his mouth. He held her ass as he made contact with her, her hands in his hair guiding him. He was afraid he was going to come just from pleasuring her. She let out a moan, and he squeezed her to him, honing in on the spot that seemed to make her happy.

She pulled away. "Get that condom."

He followed orders, and she lowered herself down onto him. Her warmth surrounding him made him feel like a whole man when he didn't even know he wasn't one.

She rode him, grinding up and down on him, rocking his whole body and his mind. He wanted more of Meade. Sex with her was gratification on a level he never knew existed. He was so overcome with emotion it was on the tip of his tongue to say he loved her. But what a stupid thing to even think at this point. He didn't know her that way. But he knew he was batshit crazy for her. There was no denying that.

"Are you ready?" she asked in that deep, breathy voice that made him insane.

"Yes," he said, squeezing her shoulders.

He loved that she wanted them to come together every time. What a treasure she was.

They let go in perfect unison and he held her against him, their breaths slowing together. He'd never felt more in sync with someone in his life. He didn't understand how he found her. But he was thankful he had. And he had no intention of letting her go.

Chapter Fifteen

Meade and Ryder made it back to the house without getting caught. Or at least it felt that way. But with the grin that would not get off her face, she knew it was just a matter of time before someone caught on.

She had sent Ryder to go find something else to do that didn't involve the two of them being around one another. Otherwise, someone was bound to figure it out just by their stupid grins.

Maya walked up to the bar and leaned against it. "How has your night been?"

"Uneventful," Meade lied.

"Same. I thought I was stuffy, but these clients of Rob's are even worse than me." Her gaze honed in on a heavyset lady with big hair and an even bigger personality. "Except for Peaches. Have you met her?"

"She told me my signature drink was her favorite thing about this night."

"She and her husband Frank are the reason Gwendolen and Rob are together, to hear her tell it."

"I can see her being a matchmaker," Meade said, grabbing a used cocktail napkin off the bar and tossing it in the trashcan.

"Would you like to come over for dinner one day this week?" Maya asked.

"Sure. I'm off at five."

"Great. Bo said he would make that salmon you like."

"That sounds good."

Maya cut her gaze at Meade briefly and then crossed her arms over her chest as she exhaled a deep breath, glancing around the room. "I saw you walking up from the boat with that guy Ryder earlier."

Meade should've known Maya would be the one to bust her. Why couldn't somebody want a drink right this second? "He was showing me the boat. It was pretty cool."

Maya trained her gaze on Meade. "Are you and he a couple?"

"God no. I'm done with the couple stuff. You know that."

"I wouldn't actually be opposed to you being coupled up with that guy. You know he's got a teenage daughter, right?"

Meade tried to refrain from rolling her eyes. "So I've heard."

Maya looked contrite. "What is going on? Are you dating him?" She leaned in. "Screwing him?"

Meade gave her a look. "Nosy much?"

"I'm your sister. You should tell me these things."

"What about you? Do you have anything to tell me? Any news?"

Maya pursed her lips and withdrew. "I think we're going to take a break from trying. And don't say that's when we'll get pregnant. I hate it when people say that, because then I'll have it in my mind that we're taking a break but we still need to try so it can accidentally happen or something like that. I just want to not think about it for a few months. But we'll start back...maybe after Christmas."

"You sound like you're making excuses. You don't ever have to start back as far as I'm concerned."

"I know. It's just frustrating. I feel like I did something to screw this up. I mean, not like to my body or anything. But waiting till I was thirty-five to get married."

"So you should've married Al and not waited like you did and ended up with the most perfect guy on the planet? Yeah, you really screwed up, Maya." Meade could not have been more thrilled when Maya broke things off with her ex, Al. He was a mouse of a man who Meade had no time for.

Maya let out an exhaustive sigh. "I know. Do you know how guilty I feel even talking like this? I know I won the lottery with Bo. I know any girl in this state would fall all over herself for one night with him much less a lifetime."

Meade lifted her eyebrows.

Maya nodded. "I know."

"You also have the right to want children," Meade said, knowing she was talking out of both sides of her mouth, but just wanting to make Maya feel better, whatever it took.

She exchanged a look with her sister, the one where they stared at each other till they both smiled. It was one of the few ways they were in sync. "Maybe I'll go home and screw his brains out but we'll use a condom just so I can enjoy it and not feel like this could be the time or anything stupid like that," Maya said.

"Whatever makes you happy, my love," Meade said.

Ryder moseyed up to the bar, setting his fist down. "Two pale ales, please. Men after my own heart. There's a couple of guys out here who started a card game. I want to keep them plowed while their wives buy lots of art."

He turned to Maya and held out his hand. "It's Maya, isn't it?"

Maya shook his hand with a skeptical look. "It is. And you're Ryder."

"Correct. He tapped the bar with both hands in a little drumbeat. He was way too happy, and Meade knew why. Only because she was just as happy but better at hiding it.

Maya gave Ryder a look. "I thought I liked you until you helped my sister sabotage her chances to work in the history department with David."

Ryder shrugged. "What can I say? She needed backup."

Meade slid the two beers toward him with a warning glance.

"I'll just get these where they need to go. Good to see you, Maya."

"Nice to see you as well."

As he walked off, Maya slid her gaze to Meade. "I am no fool."

Meade shrugged as a couple of women approached her, and Maya slipped away.

As the night breezed by, the crowd thinned, leaving just the crew who had come to help and the host and hostess. They all gravitated toward one another in the living room.

"Is it time for the after party yet?" Gwendolen asked.

Chase walked up behind Marigold, putting her in a headlock. She bit his arm and he faked pain, but his smile told otherwise. They somehow both got away with flirtations that no other coupled up people would be allowed to get by with. Chase and Marigold had been best friends before they each partnered up with their respective sweethearts. Dane, Marigold's boyfriend, must have been secure enough in his relationship with Marigold not to be too bothered by it. But Meade noticed him staring a little bit too hard at Chase. On the other hand, Shayla, Chase's wife, was the most secure woman Meade had ever been around. Meade always considered herself the laid back one in the room, but Shayla put her to shame. She was as cool as they came.

Blake put his arm around his wife, Seanna. "We haven't been to Wooley's since the night Bo kissed Sebastian on the mouth."

Meade had heard the story. It was all in fun, but it was apparently an epic moment and a story that was told often. Sebastian had been jokingly accusing Bo of being a homophobe, and Bo had proved him wrong right there on the spot.

Sebastian waggled his eyebrows, putting his hands on his hips. "I'd be up for round two of that."

Bo looked at Maya in question. She threaded her arm through Meade's. "I'll go to Wooley's. I've never been."

Meade had been a handful of times with Ashe, Ethan, and Sebastian and loved the place. Gay men on the dance floor? She was in. "I'm up for it."

Chase wrapped his arms around Shayla, putting his hands on her stomach. "This little fella is way too young for Wooley's."

Everyone gave the requisite oohs and awws while Meade squeezed her sister to her, physically feeling Maya's pain.

"We're in," said Gwendolen, glancing up at her husband with raised eyebrows.

"I don't think I've ever been to a gay bar," Rob said.

"Oh my God," Annabella said. "A gay bar?" She turned to Ryder. "Dad, please. We've got to go."

Ryder chuckled. "You're fifteen. You're not going to any bar."

"Please? Is it a restaurant too? Would they let me in?" Annabella asked the crowd at large.

"It's twenty-one and over, sweetie," Sebastian said. "But don't you worry. I will take you there personally on

119

your twenty-first birthday."

Annabella's face fell in disappointment.

"Y'all have fun," Ryder said, meeting Meade's gaze.

Damn, she wished he could be there. But this was life when you had a kid. Your life was not your own. Yet another reason why she couldn't let it get out of hand with him.

"You all are coming, aren't you?" Gwendolen asked Marigold and Desiree.

"We're on cleanup duty."

"Oh please. We'll hire a crew to come in here tomorrow," Gwendolen said.

"Absolutely not," Marigold said. "We've got this."

"Ethan and I are going to hang around and help too." Ashe said. "Y'all go though." He turned to Sebastian. "Kiss a shirtless boy for me."

Ethan raised his eyebrows, and Ashe slid his arms around Ethan's waist. "You know you're the only one I want to kiss," he said with a wink.

As part of the group dispersed to clean and the other part talked logistics, Ryder walked over to Meade, pulling her aside. "I wish I could be with you tonight," he said in a low voice.

Meade glanced around to see who was looking.

"Am I your dirty little secret?" he asked.

"No," she said, sounding like she was lying.

"Will you text me when you get home?"

"You'll be up at like two or three in the morning?" Meade asked doubtfully.

"You could wake me up from a dead sleep and I'd love it."

"You say that now…"

"Can I see you tomorrow?"

"Shouldn't you be spending the day with Annabella?"

"She's going to paint a school with a group from her school."

"Isn't she grounded?"

"The principal recommended it. It's supposed to be a group of good kids."

"What did you have in mind?" Meade asked.

"Anything you want, gorgeous."

Oh how Meade needed to get her fluttering belly under control when he said stuff like that. "I'll think about it. I'll see how tonight goes at Wooley's. I may have another date tomorrow."

He shook his head at her with a grin that let her know he knew she was lying. "Something tells me you're not gonna get me out of your head tonight."

She rolled her eyes. "Please. You don't know who you're dealing with."

"I know tonight was amazing and so was last Saturday night. I want to be with you more. And I think you want to be with me too."

She pursed her lips at him. "Don't get too cocky there, Ryder. I've told you I'm not in this for more than a fling."

"I know what you said." His mouth quirked up in a confident smile, and he turned and walked away from her.

Chapter Sixteen

There was a day just a few months ago when nothing made Meade happier than being at Wooley's with Sebastian and the rest of her new friends. Here she was on the dance floor, moving freely to one of her favorite songs, but a piece of her heart was missing. All she could think about was Ryder's cute little cocky, one-sided smile.

She got Sebastian's attention and motioned to the bar. He nodded and followed after her. She ordered a beer, her first of the evening. Since she'd been working, she hadn't been drinking, and they'd all gone directly to the dance floor as soon as they'd come in.

"What do you want?" she asked Sebastian.

"Bottle of water. DD."

She got their drinks and handed his bottle to him. He slipped the bartender the money before she had the opportunity to.

"Sebastian, you know you don't have to always pay for everything."

"What if it makes me happy?" he said, sitting on a stool with his back to the bar, facing the dance floor. She followed suit, tapping her beer against his water bottle. "Cheers."

"What are we drinking to?" he asked.

"A successful night? How did they do?"

"They did really well. That woman Peaches bought three pieces and wants to do a showing at her house and invite all her friends."

"That sounds promising."

"She and her husband are loaded. They have their own yacht."

"Good for Desiree and Marigold."

He nudged her. "So, you and Ryder, huh?"

She tried to put on a bemused face. "What are you talking about?"

"Oh please. The two of you were practically mauling each other all night."

She wondered what he'd seen. "We were not."

"You wanted to be. I've never seen two people giddier in my life. And I've never seen you look so happy."

She gave him a doubtful look. "I am not."

"Yes you are. I've known you since we were teenagers. I've never seen you like this."

"That's because usually when you see me, I'm coming off of a heartbreak of some sort."

"Maybe. Or maybe Ryder's *the one*."

"He's definitely not *the one*. He's got a fifteen-year-old daughter."

"I met her. Reminds me of someone." He lifted his eyebrows.

Meade hadn't really thought about it, but Annabella was very much like her—smart but didn't really want to be. Just wanted to be one of the popular kids and would do whatever it took to get there. Meade understood it all. "I can't get into this with him. You know me, Sebastian.

Can you imagine me being someone's mother?"

He thought about it. "To a fifteen-year-old girl who never really had a mother and needs one desperately? Absolutely."

Meade rolled her eyes, shaking her head. "I still don't have my shit together. I don't know if I ever will."

"None of us do."

"Please. You're more pulled together than anyone."

"Yeah, that's why I'm so good at relationships." He rolled his eyes at himself. Sebastian was the biggest catch Meade knew. He was handsome and financially stable, the most caring and considerate person alive. Everyone who got to know him loved him. All of them thought they were Sebastian's best friend. The truth was they all were. He gave that much of himself. But he was not lucky in love. And she knew why.

"Have you talked to your dad at all?"

He shook his head. "Not since I walked out the door the day after graduation."

Sebastian lost his mother as a small child and his father had never accepted who he was. It was a classic, tragic story, and one Meade could never understand. She knew his father when they were in high school. He was a rigid, cold man. How someone as warm and loving as Sebastian shared DNA with that man was beyond Meade.

She was pretty sure Sebastian's issues with his father were tangled up in his relationship issues. Because it wasn't like he couldn't get a date. There were plenty of men interested. Sebastian had to work it out internally before he could really put himself out there. And Meade knew she wasn't unlike him.

She thought about the billionaire beating down her door. She hadn't told anyone about the possibility of the job. Sebastian was just the right trustworthy, nonjudgmental guy to talk it out with.

She gaged him. "If I tell you something, can you keep

it a secret from Maya?"

"Of course."

She let out a sigh. "There's a job I'm considering."

"Okay."

"It's in space travel," she said, her cheeks heating.

"Like working for NASA?"

She rolled her eyes. "No. One of the stupid billionaires who wants to taxi people to space. It's ridiculous when we have people living in poverty all around us. That money should go to those people, not to these assholes' egos."

"Which billionaire?"

She pursed her lips. "Andrew Harrington."

"Wow," he said, staring at her like she was a zoo animal.

She rolled her eyes, shifting in her seat. "It's not a big deal."

"But you're still interested in the job," he said.

"Yeah. You know I don't even have my degree in astrophysics."

"I know you don't. That was such a tragedy to watch you go prelaw when we all knew space is what you were always interested in."

"It is what it is. But that's the thing. This guy doesn't really care what my degree is in. He read my paper I wrote for that professor a couple of years ago. And then he talked with my boss from the Chicago job. He's been tracking me down. It's a little stalker-ish to be honest."

Sebastian shook his head. "Sometimes I forget who you are."

His words stung. "You know who I am."

"I do. You're fun Meade. You're 'dance at Wooley's and bartend' Meade. Still, every once in a while, I forget that you're capable of things the vast majority of us can't achieve."

"That's not fair."

"I'm just being honest. I know you hate it when people

talk about how smart you are, but it's this amazing gift."

If it were anybody but Sebastian she would get up and walk away, but nobody had a heart as big as his and he'd never say anything to purposely upset her. She just looked down at her beer, running her finger through the condensation.

"Where is the job?" he asked.

"It's in Texas."

"Can you do it remotely?"

"This guy wants his team right there around him. I get it. I would too for what he's trying to do."

"When does it start?"

"As soon as I say yes."

"Before Ryder, would you have said yes?"

She lifted her chin. "I knew about it before I met the two of them." It was true, but it was also true that she'd all but put the job out of her mind since they'd been hanging out.

"How long is this billionaire going to wait for you to answer?"

"He told me he needed an answer one way or the other by the end of this month."

"That's not far away."

"I know."

"If you stay, what's the plan?"

She shrugged. "Serving margaritas on the beach."

"That job has an expiration date too, I'm guessing, with the end of the season approaching."

"There's plenty of bartender jobs in restaurants."

Sebastian cocked his head to the side, giving her a no-bullshit look. "Meade, you've got to grow up sometime."

"You know you're the only person on the planet who could get away with saying that to me."

"Why do you think I'm saying it?"

Meade's phone buzzed and she checked the screen. Ryder's name practically gave her goosebumps.

How's Wooley's? I wish I could see you on the dance floor.

She smiled at the phone, her heart thudding away. In a moment he sent another text.

Me on the other hand...

He sent a gif of Elaine from Seinfeld doing her famous thumb over the shoulder dance. She giggled, staring at the phone, thinking of how she wanted to respond.

"Yeah, he makes you pretty miserable, doesn't he?" Sebastian said, hopping down off the stool.

Meade texted back a gif of some women doing aerobics in the eighties with hilarious outfits on.

He sent back a laughing emoji and then sent a picture of the empty pillow on his bed.

Wish you were here.

She took a picture of the empty barstool next to her.

Wish you were here.

I wish I was anywhere that you were.

What if I was in prison?

That got dark fast.

She laughed and texted again.

What if I was in alligator-infested waters?

I'd want to be swimming the backstroke next to you.

She grinned.

What if I was sitting through an eight-hour lecture on molecules?

Sign me up.

She bit her lip.

What if I was on a deserted island in the Caribbean with nothing but a blanket and a smile?

Now you're talking.

He sent a gif of a cartoon character with its eyes bulging wide, and texted again.

Not being with you right now is physically paining me.

You know there are ways to relieve that pain, right?

Like I'll ever be able to satisfy myself now that I know

what being with you does to me.

She held the tip of her thumb between her teeth as she tried to think of the perfect thing to say.

Maya plopped down next to her, killing the mood. Meade clicked her screen off and pocketed her phone. "What's up?" she asked, a little abruptly. She tried again. "Are you having fun?"

"Yes, for the first time in ages. I think trying to have a baby is putting a bigger toll on me than I realized. I needed this, desperately."

Bo slid in next to Maya on the other side, whispering something into her ear that made her giggle like a girl newly in love. She turned to him, letting him slide in between her legs. They weren't kissing, but they might as well be, as close as they were talking. Meade slid off the stool and walked to an empty spot in the back of the bar. She pulled out her phone and texted.

You have some decent moves of your own.

Thank God.

She smiled.

What do you like that I do? he asked.

I can't tell you that. Then you'd overuse the move.

Or I'd be afraid to overuse it and never do it.

Exactly. That's why I have to keep you guessing.

I'm pretty good at guessing.

Oh yeah?

You have tells.

She smiled. *What tells?*

Noises you make.

Are you calling me noisy, Ryder?

I adore your noises.

Her body sizzled as she rested against a wall, staring at her phone like it was the only thing in the room. *I like your thighs. They're solid.*

That's a new one. But thanks. I like your torso.

She winced. Of all things for him to say he liked. Her

torso contained her belly which was not her favorite part of her body.

I don't think I can wait till tomorrow to see you, he texted.

I don't think you have a choice.

I've never felt so out of control with a woman. You make me feel like I've jumped out of a plane with no parachute.

This made Meade feel both powerful and ashamed at the same time. Though she liked being in control, she didn't like making Ryder feel helpless, which was what he seemed to be describing. Part of her understood exactly how he felt. She didn't want to be falling for him, but no doubt he was reeling her in. She typed back.

Isn't the fall the best part?

He sent her back a gif of a guy doing a bellyflop into a swimming pool. *Can I see you tomorrow? I drop Annabella off at nine.*

You can pick me up after that. She texted her address.

He sent her a smiley face emoji. She waited a minute, but that seemed to be the end of the conversation. It was so wrong that she wanted to text with him all night and not be on the dance floor with her friends. She was getting hooked by this guy and she was practically powerless to do anything about it.

Just as she was getting ready to go back to the dance floor, her phone buzzed.

Good night, Meade.

Her heart filled with warmth as she imagined him saying her name. She texted back.

Sweet dreams.

She pocketed her phone, putting her hand on her forehead and closing her eyes, realizing for the first time just how gone she really was.

Chapter Seventeen

When Ryder pulled up to Meade's place, she was standing on the driveway talking with a middle-aged woman and a teenage boy who looked about Annabella's age. The boy was tossing a soccer ball up in the air and moving around constantly like nervous teenage boys did. He kept looking at Meade in her casual skirt and fitted T-shirt that hugged her chest and then back at the ball. He probably had a crush on her. What straight, red-blooded American male wouldn't?

Meade was the most captivating woman Ryder had ever known. Not only was she striking with golden blond hair and soft, blue eyes, but she was intriguing in a way he never experienced from a woman. Just the way she looked at him with a hint of a smile and lazy eyes like she had a secret did him in every time. He felt like he was that kid's age around her.

Meade spotted him, gave him her signature smile with that mouth he could devour, then put her attention back on the woman who quickly caught on that Meade's date was there. She appeared to finish up what she was saying and then held up her hand to Ryder in a wave as she walked toward the house. The kid was less interested in being nice. He just stared at Ryder holding the ball on his hip.

Ryder got out of the car and met Meade. "You look really good."

"As opposed to my black bartender uniform last night?"

"You looked good in that too."

She just smiled at him. "Are you ready?"

"I don't get to see your apartment?"

"There's really not a lot to see."

"I was hoping to get a glimpse into your life in there."

She gave him a doubtful look. "You weren't just wanting to go in there so you could toss me in the bed?"

"I definitely want to do that too. But I also want to see into the real you."

"No, you don't."

"Oh yes I do."

She gave him that lazy smile. "Let's get out of here before this gets out of hand."

"Out of hand is what we do best," he said, walking her to the passenger side. As he opened the door for her, he couldn't think of any way he'd rather spend his day than with her.

"Where are we going?" she asked as he strapped himself in.

"I have a couple of ideas. We could either go shopping at Pier Park and to a movie, or we could go to this science museum." He showed her his phone where he'd pulled it up. "Have you been?"

"No," she said, her brow furrowed.

"It's a bit of a drive, but I hear it's worth it."

She scrolled through the website, frowning.

"Pier Park it is," he said, backing out of the driveway.

She bit her lip and let out a sigh. "Okay. We can do the museum."

He glanced over at her as she stared pensively out the window. "We really don't have to."

"No, we can. It looks interesting. Though it's probably really for kids, right?"

"I think most of these museums are for kids. But that doesn't mean they're not cool and interesting."

She shrugged.

He stopped at a red light and handed her his phone. "I made a playlist of women in rock last night. See how I did. You can grade me."

She cut her eyes at him. "Everything is not academic."

"I know. But this feels a little like a test, even though it's self-inflicted."

"Are you a masochist, Ryder?"

"I wanted you to have music you liked for the drive."

She gave him a curious look that he couldn't really read so he kept talking, a nervous habit he couldn't break, especially around her. "You can introduce me to some new stuff. Clearly, I know all the big names. Tina Turner, Pat Benatar, Blondie. That first day we talked at the library and then went out to eat, you had on that T-shirt that had Liz Phair on it. I had heard of her, but I didn't really know any of her songs."

She scrolled and then looked up at him with that accusatory smile. "Fuck and Run?"

"It was her second most popular song. I liked the most popular one too, but this one was a little more interesting."

She shrugged. "Accurate."

"The other most popular song also had the F bomb in it. She really likes to use that word, doesn't she?"

"Is there something wrong with fuck?"

"No, not at all. Except that I usually try not to say it around Annabella...or at work. That really narrows the opportunities. I guess I've gotten out of the habit. Now it just sounds kind of awkward coming from me."

She stared at him, the smile widening her face.

"What?" he asked, trying to get his own smile under control.

"Nothing," she said, but it was definitely something.

Ryder knew Meade would never admit to it, but she was like a kid in a candy store at the science museum. She took her time at every exhibit, asking the guides genuine questions, though most of them seemed to go right over their heads.

As their path around the museum took them toward the planetarium, Ryder could feel Meade's excitement radiating off her in her cool, calm way.

"Do you want to go to a show?" he asked.

A guide shouted from the doorway, "Next show in five minutes."

They slid into the line that had formed, and Meade turned to him. "Thank you for planning this. It's been forever since I've been to one of these places."

"I'm glad you're liking it."

"I can't remember coming to one of these since maybe I was in grade school. I always thought I'd take Maya's kids to these kinds of places, but we know the story there."

"How is she doing?"

"I'm not sure. She and Bo are solid. But I know it's taking a toll on her. It's frustrating. I wish there was something I could do to help." The deep scowl on Meade's face revealed how much she truly loved her sister.

"You never wanted a family? Not even a little?"

She shook her head as they moved forward in line. "My dreams were always in the stars."

It was on the tip of his tongue to ask her more about why she didn't pursue a career in astrophysics, but he knew better. He thought of what Bo had said last night about not making any big sudden moves. He'd been doing that, but in a flirtatious way and talking about the one subject that was on the table between the two of them, sex. For some reason, that felt appropriate. But anything about her private life, including her career notions, and he might as well be blowing a foghorn.

They headed inside and took their seats. As the show started and they leaned back, looking up at the stars, Ryder recalled the handful of times he'd done this kind of show, including with Annabella. It had always been scientific for him, a cool learning experience. But somehow sitting next to Meade, it felt like they were on the moon together looking up at their own universe.

The recorded voice came on, guiding them through the show with the planets and the stars and the moon. He kept sneaking glances at Meade who was gazing upward with her mouth open and wonder in her eyes. As they watched planets rotating around the sun, Meade reached over and took Ryder's hand in hers. They'd been inside one another and had done intimate acts that required full trust. Yet somehow this felt like the most risqué thing they had done yet.

As they drove back through Panama City, focused on the playlist Ryder had made, he thought about how the vibe had shifted in the past twenty-four hours. Last night they had been flirtatious and even had sex on a boat that didn't belong to them. But today, Meade was not her provocative self. He was getting to see the academic side of her for the first time.

He felt honored that she would let him in this way, but he didn't know how to approach this Meade. When it was only about sex, he knew exactly how to play her game. She liked him aggressive and amorous...had no problem with him making moves on her verbally or physically. But he didn't get the signals from her today that she was open for that. Her mood was different. She was more like a coworker he had a huge crush on but couldn't approach.

He glanced down at the clock on his dash which read four-nineteen. "I've got to pick up Annabella at five," he said.

Meade nodded.

"Would you like to come with me? We could go out to dinner, the three of us."

She seemed to consider it. "No, that's okay. You should be with her."

"You know she'd rather be with you than me."

"You need time with her alone."

As much as he knew she was right, he couldn't stand the thought of ending this day with her.

"I know we're short on time, but can I come in and see your place?"

She cut her eyes at him. "That's really important to you, isn't it?"

"I wanna see where you live."

"There's not much to see. It's one room with a tiny kitchen area and a bathroom."

"I don't care what color your dishes are. I just want to see the little bits of you."

"Get ready for major disappointment." They pulled into her driveway and the kid that had been outside with her earlier had multiplied. There were two of him.

He remembered her mentioning twin boys that lived next-door to her the night she was trying to help Annabella respond to Grace's texts. "These are the boys you mentioned to Annabella the other night, aren't they?"

"Yep."

"How old are they?"

"Sixteen. Their mom is freaking out because they're driving now. She says she feels like she's pushing them out on the highway on a tricycle."

Ryder did not see little boys when he looked at these

two. He saw kids who could possibly humiliate his daughter and make her lash out in ways that worried him to death.

"I think the one who was here when I picked you up has a crush on you."

She looked at him like he was crazy. "Why would you say that?"

"Do you think I can't spot a teenage boy with a crush? I was one."

She rolled her eyes and they both got out of the car.

"Meade," one of them yelled in a voice lower than Ryder's own, which irritated him. "My mom put a piece of mail on your doorstep. Hope an alligator didn't crawl up and get it."

His brother threw a ball at him and he caught it. "There's not any alligators around here, dumbass."

The boy threw the ball back and it wasn't long before they were wrestling on the ground.

"Is there an age when that stops?" Meade asked as they walked to her back door.

"I don't know. I never had a brother."

Meade picked up the envelope, reviewing it with interest. It wasn't something that came through the mail. It was a cardboard sleeve delivered overnight. She let them into the house, dropping the envelope face down on a small table that sat next to the door. It was all he could do not to ask what it was.

She held her arms out. "I know. It's fascinating."

Ryder took his focus off the envelope and put it on the room as a whole. This was where she lived. This was Meade all around him. For some reason, he had been expecting a big bookshelf full of books, but there was nothing like that. No pictures on the walls. Her bed had no headboard or footboard. Just a mattress and box springs shoved against a wall. There was no television in the room, just a cozy chair in a corner with a blanket puddled on the cushion. "Is that where you read?" he asked.

"Most of the time. Sometimes I read in bed."

"You don't have a television?"

"If I want to watch something I do it on my phone."

It dawned on Ryder how few possessions Meade had. He understood now why she spent so much time at the library. She didn't want to collect books. She just wanted to read them and return them. She didn't want to collect anything. This was a woman who wanted to be mobile. Ryder's heart seized as he realized just how fragile the state of their relationship was.

He picked up the book she had on her nightstand, expecting to find something brainy. He looked at her. "A romance novel?"

"Yeah. I like romance novels."

He nodded, loving this about her. She was a romantic? She liked to read stories about two people falling in love? It didn't fit her tough exterior and her no-relationship rule.

"I know you're not making fun of romance novels," she said.

"No, not at all. Millions of readers can't be wrong. It's just not what I expected out of you."

"You don't know me, Ryder."

"Why do you think I wanted in here?"

She tossed her hands up. "This is it. This is me. Not too interesting, I know."

He walked over to her and put his hands on her hips. "I think you're the most fascinating woman I've ever come into contact with."

"What a boring life you've lived."

"There's nothing boring about my life right now," he said, tucking her curl behind her ear. Her hair was baby fine and so soft.

"You've got to go get your daughter," she said, her voice shaky. Was he making her nervous?

"I've got a few minutes."

"I don't want to be your quickie."

He ran his hands over her ass, drawing her to him. "I know I have obstacles in my life, but I want to make the most of every single moment I have with you, even if it is only twenty minutes. I want some of those minutes inside of you."

She inhaled a sharp intake of breath, which gave him the confidence to reach down and kiss her. He knew what she liked by now. She had ways of telling him without speaking any words. He moved his hand underneath her shirt to the small of her back, rubbing his thumb up and down, making her kiss him harder. She liked that for some reason, though he couldn't understand why.

He nudged her over to the bed, hovering over her as he kissed her. She scooted up on the bed and he moved with her, tugging her skirt and panties down past her hips. He slid between her legs, and she gripped his arms as he moved in on her. He savored every moment of her pleasure as she gasped and squirmed and then finally gave in to him.

As she lay on the bed catching her breath, the back of her hand covering her eyes, he took off his shorts, pulling the condom he'd stowed away out of his pocket. He readied himself and then climbed back on top of her. As he entered her, she let out his favorite moan.

"I love it when you make that noise," he said, pushing into her.

"I didn't make a noise. You made a noise," she said with a smile.

He shut up and did his thing, making sure to last longer than usual in case she could come again. After a while, she squeezed his arms. "Let go."

He followed her instructions and collapsed on top of her. He kissed her neck, and then took her earlobe between his teeth and tugged on it. She laughed as he rolled off of her.

She smiled at him with unspoken words, and then finally said, "I don't like it when you break my rules."

"You could've said no at any time."

She closed her eyes, letting a hard breath out, and then sat up and got dressed. He went to the bathroom to pull himself together. He splashed water on his face, gauging himself in the mirror. He had to walk away from her now and go be a dad. He hoped he was saying and doing all the right things to keep her around. But he had no clue what he was doing. Sex was his only solid form of communication.

He walked out to the main room and found her at a mini fridge pulling out a couple of bottles of water. She handed him one. "Thank you for the date. I had a good time."

"I did too. I want to see you again."

She let out a sigh, looking down. "I'll text you."

His heart sank. "Why do I feel like that's a lie?"

She met his gaze. "I told you I don't do relationships."

"What if I said I just wanted to see you for sex?"

"I'd call you a liar."

She put on a stern face, but he was getting to know all of her tells, and he could see clearly when her words didn't match her thoughts.

"Is it really the worst thing in the world for us to have a relationship?"

She shook her head. "This is getting into dangerous territory."

He put his hands on her shoulders. "Why is it so dangerous?"

"You know why. I'm not a mom and I'm not a wife either." She looked away, and he followed her gaze to the envelope on the table.

"Is there something important in that envelope?"

She sighed. "I honestly don't know what's in there."

"But you have an idea."

She held his gaze in challenge. "You've got to go get your daughter."

"Meade, what's in that envelope?"

She lifted her chin, standing up straight. "It's something I'm considering."

He nodded, the possibilities swirling through his brain, none of them good. "Will you tell me when you're ready?"

"I'll tell you when there's something to tell. For now, go get your daughter." She walked over to the door and opened it for him, gripping the door knob as she leaned against it.

He nodded and then cupped his hand on the nape of her neck. He reached down and gave her a slow, deliberate kiss intended to linger with her after he was gone. When he pulled away her eyes remained closed, and he knew all he could do now was hope. "See you, Meade," he said, and walked away.

Chapter Eighteen

Meade closed the door and leaned against it before collapsing to the floor. She was not a crier. Meade Forbes never cried. So, what was this stupid liquid coming from her eyes?

She'd known what she was getting into with Ryder. She'd been saying from the jump that she was not going to get sucked in, but here she was…completely sucked.

She could not have orchestrated a better date herself. The man had found her favorite songs and put them on a playlist, for God's sake. And then he'd taken her to the one magical place she hadn't allowed herself to go back to since she was a kid.

Her parents had driven the words *law school* into her brain from the time she could talk. While she'd always loved outer space, going to school for astrophysics hadn't been a thought in her brain, until she had gone to the science museum on a field trip in the fifth grade. Meade knew what she wanted to do with her life right then.

She could not even comprehend the irony of it. Ryder

was single-handedly pulling her to the surface, showing her what she needed to do, which did not include him in the plan.

She grabbed the envelope from the table and ripped it open. It was a check for ten grand with a note on it that said *Contemplation Bonus. Yours whether or not you take the job.*

That fucking billionaire. He was relentless, tossing money at her like she was a whore. Not that she couldn't use it. Life on 30A wasn't cheap and her credit card balance was starting to build.

She took a picture of the check and deposited it on the banking app on her phone right then and there. Of course she'd take his money. Did he think this was some kind of test of her integrity? He should know right away who he was dealing with. He'd learn quickly that this didn't mean she was beholden to him or obligated to take the job. Meade could walk away. It was what she did best.

The ding of Meade's text alert tone caused her to blink awake. She had no idea how long she'd been asleep. Could've been half an hour. Could've been three days.

The time on her phone let her know it had been twelve hours. She couldn't remember the last time she'd had that much sleep. Of course, the bottle of wine she drank may have had something to do with that.

The name on her screen was one she hadn't seen in a while. Felicity Haley had been her sister's friend originally. Maya, Sebastian, and Felicity had been BFFs all through high school. Meade supposed she had been the cool, older sister that they'd all tried to emulate. But only in the older teenage years, because God knew Meade had been a geek before her sixteenth birthday.

Meade had known Felicity all these years but they'd never been close until around the time Maya had gotten with Bo. Meade had fled Las Vegas to meet Maya and

Felicity at Sebastian's house here in Florida, then she had ridden home with the two of them. Once back in Indy, Meade and Felicity had grown closer during the short time Meade lived there before she left for Chicago. Once Meade had gotten to know Felicity outside of her relationship with Maya, she had wished they'd gotten closer sooner. When they were younger, the two-year age gap had been in the way, but such things didn't matter in your thirties.

Felicity and Meade had a lot in common. Both were single girls in their mid-to-late thirties, neither one having much interest in settling, and neither one wanting kids. They were unicorns. They would've grown even closer had Meade not moved to Chicago.

Felicity's first text read: *I have some news. I'm actually here in Florida.*

The second one read: *I've been hiding at Sebastian's house for a couple of days. I made him keep my secret.*

And then finally: *I could use a friend and a stiff drink. Are you busy tonight?*

The texts had been sent half an hour ago. Meade sat up and focused on the phone, tapping into it.

I have no plans. I would love a drink and some company.

Meade wasn't so sure about that drink part at the moment, but she had rallied before and she would rally again.

Perfect. Where do you live? I will come to you. I'm not fit for public consumption right now, and I think that thing about houseguests starting to stink after three days is ringing true. Can I stay over tonight?

I live in a three-hundred-square-foot room with a full-sized bed. But you are welcome.

See you at six? I'll bring the food.

I'll have the wine.

When Felicity showed up, Meade barely recognized her. Felicity usually looked like something out of a Hollywood movie. She typically had every part of her body ready for the runway from her fingernails down to her bikini line. She lived in spas where she got facials, pedicures, waxes, and treatments Meade didn't know how to pronounce. Standing here at Meade's backdoor was a woman with her auburn hair tucked up in a ponytail with Coke bottle glasses and chipped nail polish. Meade wanted to look behind this woman to see where Felicity was.

She pulled Felicity into a hug. "It's good to see you, friend."

Felicity chuckled as she walked in. "Is it ridiculous that I still get all tingly that you wanna be my friend?"

Meade rolled her eyes. "That's a delusion from childhood. You'll get over it quickly. Have a seat." She offered her the chair as she sat down on the edge of the bed.

Felicity tossed up her hands. "I forgot the food. Fuck."

"I've got a phone. We've got food."

Felicity plopped down in the chair. "Fuck my life."

Meade narrowed her gaze, wondering if it was possible that Felicity was even more messed up than she was. "What's going on with you?"

"I'll just go ahead and rip the bandage off. I finally got my mom to leave my dad."

Meade's jaw dropped. This was huge news. Felicity had wanted to leave Indy ever since she was in high school. And Maya and Sebastian had wanted her down here in Florida since the day Maya moved down here. But everyone knew that Felicity would never leave Indy because of her mother. Felicity's father had been abusive to her mother their whole life. Felicity had gone through painstaking efforts and programs and therapists trying to get her mother to leave him. She had been beholden to Indy and to her parents' relationship her whole life.

"That's great news, isn't it?"

Felicity rubbed her forehead. "I thought it was. I thought I had finally gotten through after all these years. I thought all this work, all this staying put in a city I hate and turning down jobs and opportunities and friends and vacations, and she had finally listened to me. But then I find out she's moved this guy in with her. And wouldn't you know, I meet her for lunch, and she's got a fucking black eye."

Meade covered her mouth, unable to believe this news. Suddenly her problems seemed insignificant. "I'm so sorry."

Felicity shook her head. "I would start crying right now if I had any tears left." She met Meade's gaze with wide eyes. "I can't go back. I just can't. I can't continue the cycle. I can't start it with another man. I love my mother more than anything in the world, but I can't..." She dropped off, putting her head in her hand.

Meade walked over, squeezing into the chair with her and bringing her into her chest. She just held Felicity there while she cried.

She finally got a hold of herself. "I've given up everything. I just can't do it anymore."

"You don't need to feel bad about that," Meade said.

Felicity let out a sigh as if the world was bearing down on her shoulders.

"We need wine," Meade said, her second wind coming.

"I haven't even had any wine since I've been here. All those expensive bottles lined up in Sebastian's wine rack, and I haven't had any wine. I've just been sitting around feeling like shit...feeling like the worst daughter in the world, but knowing I can't keep enabling her."

Meade pulled the corkscrew out of the drawer and opened a bottle. She knew Felicity liked this kind and this brand from when they hung this time last year. She walked the glass over to Felicity and handed it to her wordlessly.

"Thank you," Felicity said, taking a sip. "I don't mean to unload on you."

"To be honest, it's a good change of pace for me."

"What's been going on with you?" Felicity asked.

"Nothing like this. Trust me."

"Something's going on. Please. I'm begging you to tell me. I've got to get my mind off of this even if for just tonight."

Meade took her first sip of wine, wondering if she could even finish the glass. She still wasn't feeling great from last night. "It's not a new story. I'm bad with men. Try to hide your shocked face."

"God, the two of us are a motley pair, aren't we? I couldn't suck worse with men. I'm constantly suspicious of them, so afraid I'm going to get into the same pattern my mom is in."

Meade just stared at Felicity, listening.

Felicity shook her head. "Sorry, I didn't mean to make that about me. Please, tell me about this man."

"There's nothing to tell. He's a marine biologist and he has a fifteen-year-old kid."

Felicity blinked. "Wow. Sorry, but that doesn't sound like you at all."

"Ya think?"

"So, you're dating him?"

"You know I can't be with somebody like that."

"Is the kid a boy or a girl?"

"Girl."

"Oh fuck. A fifteen-year-old girl. Can you imagine? Is she a good kid?"

Meade smiled. "She reminds me of myself."

"Ah, so a whole lotta trouble, right?"

"She's me before I kissed half the sophomore class on my sixteenth birthday. She wants to be popular. She'll do anything for it. And it's not working out for her."

Felicity squirmed in her chair. "Boy, do I remember those days."

"It seems like a world ago, doesn't it?" Meade asked.

"Seems like three days ago to me. I think it's because I never got out from underneath my parents. Sorry, there I go again."

"You go all you want," Meade said. "We've got all night."

"We've got all month. I'm not going back there."

Meade sat up. "Are you serious?"

"I can't. I let my boss know. I told him I would work remotely but I wasn't coming back."

"What did he say to that?"

"Said I needed to be in the office or give my notice."

"What did you do?"

"I'm working my two-week notice out remotely."

Meade blinked. "I think you're turning into me."

"Watch out, world." The two of them laughed and held up their glasses in a toast without touching them.

Meade took a drink and then stared at Felicity. "You're here at the exact right time. I needed this distraction, badly."

"How badly? I've got to get out of Sebastian's house. I can't stand how nice he is to me. It's making me feel like shit."

"Have you told my sister that you're staying?"

"No, she's got enough on her plate with the miscarriages and…" Felicity trailed off, looking guilty.

"And me?"

Felicity gave Meade a look. "You know how your sister is. She takes responsibility for you and your life. No clue why she does that. I've told her a million times that you're a grown ass woman and can handle yourself."

"You could tell her a million more and it would never make a dent."

"I know. I'm not ready to tell Maya yet. I'll tell her. Let me just be here a little longer."

"We can go tomorrow and get a twin air mattress. I think we can fit one over there." Meade pointed beside the bed.

"Or we could go shopping for a two-bedroom apartment," Felicity said.

Meade thought about the job in Texas and Ryder and how she didn't know if she could stay here even through the month.

"Let's just get you a place to sleep here for now while we figure things out."

"Works for me if it's okay with you."

"It's more than okay with me. We can job hunt together. I've only got till the end of this month at my bartender job. The season is coming to a close."

"Well then, let's see what we can scrounge up."

"Sounds like a plan."

"And as soon as we quit drowning our sorrows, maybe we can muster up some trouble," Felicity said with a look in her eye that Meade recognized.

Just a few weeks ago, Meade would have loved seeing that look, which meant the two of them fixed up and out on the town, meeting guys. But the only man Meade could let anywhere near her heart was the one man she couldn't have.

She smiled for her friend. "Deal."

Chapter Nineteen

Ryder had been good. He'd left Meade alone for the past two weeks. He had all but convinced himself that he was going to have to let her go until this morning happened. He checked his phone when he woke up, hoping for a text like he did every day. Finally, he'd gotten the golden egg—a missed call from her.

She'd called him at twelve-thirty-seven A.M. His heart leapt when he saw he had a voicemail from her, but when he went to check it, all he heard was background noise and a female voice that was not Meade's saying, "What are you doing?" Then it cut off. It'd been a long time, but Ryder knew a drunk dial when he heard one.

No doubt she woke up this morning regretful of having called him. But the damage had been done. Or the opposite of damage if you asked Ryder. She missed him. She tried to call him and some friend of hers stopped her from leaving a message. This was all the fuel he needed to plow forward. He now had hope.

He knew better than to call her back. If she wanted to

talk to him today, she would've called. But when people get drunk, they become honest. Meade had shown her true feelings with that call to him.

As he pulled into the parking lot of Cafe 30A, his chest panged with a twinge of guilt. He missed Desiree and wanted to see her. He wanted to hear all about her art shows and the success of her business with Marigold. But he was on a fishing expedition. There was no question about that.

He found Desiree and Ashe already seated. One rarely went anywhere without the other. Ryder thought that might change once Ashe was hooked up with Ethan, but these two were as strong as ever.

He hugged both of them and then took a seat across from them, viewing them as a couple even though one was a gay man and one was a straight woman.

Ashe look him up and down with interest. "Ryder with a Y. How are you, my man?"

If Ryder didn't know Ashe, he would think that Ashe was coming on to him. But this was Ashe's way. He was flirtatious, pretty much with everyone he was around. He had this way of making you feel like you were the best-looking, most interesting guy in the room. Who wouldn't like that?

"Better now that my daughter is off being grounded. That two-week period was rough. If you've never been confined with a huffy teenager for two weeks, you haven't lived."

"I don't know how you do it," Ashe said.

"With plenty of patience," Desiree said, giving Ryder her knowing smile.

They ordered drinks and appetizers, and then Ryder gave his attention to Desiree. "Tell me all about your business. It seems to be really taking off."

Desiree plunged in with Ashe doing a lot of the talking. He was like a proud dad or a loving brother. Or maybe a doting husband? Ryder couldn't figure out their relationship. He quit trying after a handful of times hanging with them.

Ryder asked him about his photography business, and Ashe gave a handful of highlights in under twenty seconds and then leaned in. "I'm more interested in you." He waggled his eyebrows. "What's happening with you and Meade? A few weeks ago at Gwendolen and Rob's house, the two of you were like a couple of teenagers who just discovered sex."

Ryder chuckled. "I don't know about that."

"I do," Ashe said. "Spill."

Ryder wanted to make sure he was using this moment in the most advantageous way. He shrugged like it was no big deal. "Honestly, she pulled away from me after that night. We went on a date the next day, which I thought went great, but..." He trailed off, taking a drink of his beer.

Ashe and Desiree exchanged a knowing look.

Ryder had to play it cool, but that was easier said than done. "Have you seen her much?"

"We've seen her," Ashe said, considering Desiree. She lifted a shoulder in concession, and then Ashe leaned in even farther. "She asked us about you."

"When was this?" Ryder asked, unable to help himself.

Desiree drew her eyebrows together, looking at Ashe. "Wednesday night?"

"It was Thursday. Sebastian had us over. Their friend Felicity is in town. She's been staying with Meade."

Ryder didn't know any Felicity. "That sounds...nice."

"What was funny was she didn't ask about you until it was almost time to leave," Ashe said. "It was like she was holding back the whole night and couldn't help herself."

Desiree gave Ashe a look. "You certainly are reading into that quite a bit."

"I can draw conclusions. I'm very observant."

She rolled her eyes. "It was at the end of the night, and she did seem kind of interested to get the information."

Ryder wanted to ask exactly what she had said about him, but he was starting to feel like a seventh grader.

Ashe sat back and wagged his finger. "She's not over you."

"Oh hell no," Desiree said.

Ryder refrained from letting through a triumphant smile. "Good to know."

The food came and they all dug in, leaving Ryder's brain swirling with ideas. "Is she still working at the bar?"

"Not the one on the beach," Ashe said. "Bo got her a job at Alligator Alley." He leaned in again like he had a big secret. "Apparently that didn't go over well with Maya."

"Why is that?" Ryder asked, concerned. "What is Alligator Alley?"

"It's a bar in PCB," Desiree said. "Bo and Chase used to go there all the time before they became old married men."

"Apparently," Ashe said, "Bo had gone in there for a drink and ran into Meade who was in there with Felicity. He was talking Meade up to the bartender who was a buddy of his and the guy offered her a job. When Bo got home, he bragged about it to Maya, and she was furious. She wants Meade working for NASA or something. Not tending bar."

Ryder found Ashe's reference to NASA too curious to be a coincidence.

Desiree gave Ashe a look. "How do you know all that?"

"You know you can't hiccup in this group without us all knowing the cadence."

She shrugged and then gave Ryder a smile.

"Has she thought about working for NASA?" Ryder

asked.

"Oh no. I just was trying to think of somewhere smart," Ashe said. "Anyway, Alligator Alley." He lifted an eyebrow. "Just sayin'."

After Ryder said his goodbyes to Desiree and Ashe, he sat in the car in the parking lot of the restaurant, deciding whether he should go to Alligator Alley tonight or not. His daughter was safely tucked away at a new friend's house, one she had met on the trip to paint the school. The drunk dial had been last night, less than twenty-four hours ago. A lot could happen in little over twenty-four hours. What did he have to lose?

He drove down 30A, making his way to Highway 98. He'd never driven across town to go to a bar. Bars were somewhere you went because they were near your house and convenient. He certainly didn't drive half an hour to get to one...until now.

He parked in the lot of the bar, which seemed like somewhere locals would go with its gravel lot, nondescript sign, and lack of a T-shirt shop.

When he opened the door, the room was a little bigger than he expected with pool tables and dartboards in the back and 38 Special beaming from a mediocre sound system somewhere. A quick glance around revealed a handful of men and women who looked like they never left nineteen-eighty-five, except one attractive woman with auburn hair who was holding court on a barstool flanked by men on either side who were hanging on her every word.

He wondered for a moment if he'd come on a night when Meade wasn't working. The sound of a door shutting got his attention, and Meade made her way from a small hallway to the bar, checking her phone as she walked with purpose. She lifted a door on the counter, scooting inside without even noticing him, walked over to the auburn-haired girl, and handed her something.

"Thank you, my love," the woman said to Meade, reaching over the bar and planting a kiss on Meade's cheek, which left a red mark in the perfect shape of a kiss. Meade just smiled and grabbed two glasses sitting on the bar, submerging them into partially soapy water.

"Hel-lo. Who's this?" the auburn-haired woman said, staring directly at Ryder.

Meade turned to look and stopped in her tracks. Color flooded her cheeks, and he knew even though he'd made the move to come here, he had the upper hand. He wasn't the one who had drunk dialed. Cell phones could be sons of bitches to your privacy, but he was thankful for them right now.

Ryder walked to the bar, positioning himself on a stool near enough to the redhead to hold a conversation. He could tell he was in for a wild ride with her, and Meade was going to have a front row seat. He better get his game face on.

Meade took her time washing the glasses, a few times if he was counting properly.

"Meade, you have a customer. A cute one," the auburn-haired girl said.

Meade gave her a look, set her gaze on Ryder, and walked over. She was wearing a tank top and short shorts that exposed the thighs he'd been dreaming about for weeks.

She tossed a napkin on the bar and put her hands on her hips. "What are you drinking?"

"I think you know what I like."

She rolled her eyes, walked over, and pulled him a pale ale. The auburn-haired girl watched Ryder and Meade with interest.

"Do me next," the moron sitting next to the girl said. "What do I like?"

The woman backhanded the guy. "Hush. I think we've

got a situation here. Meade, is this a friend of yours?"

Meade just set the beer down in front of Ryder, holding his stare. They were playing a game of chicken, and he wouldn't back down if a herd of buffalo busted into this bar. "Happy hour's over, so you're probably just gonna want to finish that and head out," Meade said to Ryder.

"Are you sure that's what you want me to do?"

"We missed happy hour," a dumbass on the other side of the redhead said. "I want my two for one."

"You two go get a game of pool started. I'll be over there in just a minute," the woman said, dismissing the two goons. They followed her directions, getting up from the bar and heading off to the back.

The girl had still not taken her eyes off of Meade and Ryder. "Let me guess." The girl narrowed her gaze at him. "Ryder with a Y."

He had to refrain from puffing out his chest. Meade had told her friend about him. Or actually, maybe it was Ashe. He'd used that same phrase when he greeted him at dinner earlier. Maybe they'd all been talking about him at the get-together Desiree and Ashe told him about.

Meade rolled her eyes and walked away, lifting the door of the bar up and walking out into the room, picking up glasses off tables. Ryder turned to the redhead. "I'm guessing you're Felicity."

"I see our reputations precede both of us." She nodded in Meade's direction. "You found her."

"I didn't have to be much of a detective. The people in this circle of friends like to blab."

"That's for damn sure. Have you been around these people much?"

"A bit."

"They're the gossipy-ist group of people. They're also the best friends I've ever come across."

He thought about how kind Desiree had always been

to him. "I'd agree with that."

"Good, there's one thing we can agree upon."

"I'm curious, were you the one who stopped her from leaving me a message when she drunk dialed me last night?"

Felicity grinned. "Ah. I didn't catch her in time. So that's why you're here."

He shrugged fake indifference.

"I've got to give you some credit. You've got some gumption. You tracked her down and showed up. You gained a few points with me."

"I guess that's a start." He leaned in. "Would it really be the worst thing in the world if she were in a relationship with me?"

Felicity sat back, reviewing him. "I never said it would be a problem for me. I'm just abiding by her wishes."

"And what were those?"

"To keep her from calling you."

His heartbeat thudded. "Now why would she need your help with that?"

Felicity's eyes cut over to Meade who was in the back of the room, talking to a bar patron, one hand on her hip and the other holding two mugs. She glanced over at them with curiosity. Felicity smiled. "That's my girl right there. If you think I'm going to give away any of her secrets, you're not nearly as smart as your fancy degree would allude to."

"You know about my degree? What else has she told you about me?"

Her grin widened. "Wouldn't you like to know."

He took a drink of his beer, recalibrating. This girl was on her game. He wasn't used to having conversations like this. He never earned over a C minus in innuendo.

Felicity looked him up and down with interest, and he found himself sitting up straighter, wanting her approval. "I think I get all the fuss now," she said. "You're cute.

And I'm guessing you're good for my girl." She stood up from the stool, taking her glass. "Nice move coming here tonight. I hope I see more of you."

"Same."

"Good luck. You're gonna need it."

She started to walk away, but he said, "Any advice?"

"Don't give up," she said with a wink and headed off.

Chapter Twenty

Meade wiped down tables, checked on people, and did everything she could to avoid walking back behind that bar. She couldn't believe she had weakened to the point of calling Ryder last night. The sad part was she had been mostly sober. But her call had been enough to summon him here.

A sunburnt couple walked in and sat down at the bar, too happy not to be tourists. They glanced around as if looking for someone to get them a drink. She made her way back to the bar, each step making her stomach flounder harder.

She set down some dirty glasses and wiped her hands on a towel she kept behind the bar. She walked over to them and took their orders, pouring each of them a mojito. After she served their drinks, she walked over to Ryder, ready to face the music. He just stared at her with that smile that made her rethink all of her life choices.

She put her hand on her hip, shifting her weight to one side. "It was a butt dial."

He narrowed his gaze at her. "Are you sure about that? Because your friend just confirmed it was a drunk dial."

She found Felicity at the back of the bar in full "Felicity" mode, flirting and having guys dote on her.

"I was trying to call Ryan Gosling."

He quirked a smile, nodding. "Women often confuse the two of us."

She rolled her eyes at him, trying to hold back her own smile.

He leaned in. "You know, it's okay if you missed me."

"I did not miss you," she said deliberately, looking him in the eye, lying through her teeth.

"Of course you didn't. And I didn't miss you either."

She walked over and grabbed the empty glasses, putting them down in the water to wash them. "Shouldn't you be off swimming with the dolphins or something?"

"They've given me the night off. I'm landlocked for the weekend. I'm also solo tonight. Annabella's at a friend's house."

She looked up at him with her eyebrows drawn together. "I know you're not trying to get me in bed because of logistics."

"I'm trying to get you in bed because I'm going fucking crazy without you."

Her heart skipped three beats as she met his dead serious gaze, her hands submerged in dishwasher.

He stood up, tossing a bill on the bar. He walked over to where she was, leaning over the bar to meet her face-to-face. "I'm going home, and I'm gonna wait up for you, all night long if I have to. But I want you in my bed tonight." He cupped the back of her neck and pulled her in for a kiss that made her body tingle from head to toe. He drew back and met her gaze. "My door will be open. Just come on in." He walked away, leaving her standing helpless as a damsel tied to railroad tracks.

Felicity walked up to the bar. "Call me crazy, but I'd

deal with some baggage for those lips. He's pretty fantastic."

Meade gave her a skeptical look. "How do you know? You talked to him like two seconds."

"I know these things. And I know you. This isn't some worthless guy who's a drain on your finances and your intelligence. This is a hot, sweet guy who adores you. I want this for you."

Meade wiped off her hands. "I've got that job offer in Texas. I decided to take it. I'm going to call the guy tomorrow." She'd mentioned the job offer to Felicity, she'd just left out a few minor details, like it was working on a space program and Andrew Harrington would be her boss.

"Mmm-hmm. And how long do you think you'll stay there? Two months this time? Three?"

The truth of Felicity's words pierced her heart. "It's different this time," Meade said, not even convincing herself.

"Oh yeah? It's different from all the other jobs you took like this and then left a few months later? A few weeks later in some cases. Meade, I'm not gonna stand here and let you fuck this up with that guy. I've let you fuck it up with all the other ones, no problem. But this one? This is a once-in-a-lifetime opportunity. I'm not saying you shouldn't put career first. You absolutely should put it at the top on your list. But I'm not gonna sit here and encourage you to take a job that I know you're going to leave to drive to New York and wait tables at some dive, or go to Miami and be a salsa dance instructor. You leave jobs and cities. You leave people. I think what scares you the most about this guy is that you might want to stay around."

Meade could feel the pressure building at the backs of her eyes.

"Give this a chance. If you don't, you're always going

to wonder what could've happened."

"Felicity," a guy shouted from the back of the room. "We're waiting on you," he said with waggling eyebrows.

"Think about it," Felicity said as she walked away.

Chapter Twenty-One

When Meade got to Ryder's house, the door was standing open as promised. She thought he meant it figuratively.

She reviewed her state of dress and being. She had debated going home, showering, and changing into some fabulous outfit, but she just wanted to be here. And she didn't think he would care. But now that she stood in front of the screen door, she found herself questioning everything.

She was about to chicken out when he appeared, coming around the corner, wearing nothing but a pair of athletic shorts. He wasn't fighting fair. His chest was just standing there looking at her, wanting to be licked.

He pushed open the screen door, giving her an opening to walk in. She looked down at the floor as she walked into his house, feeling like a high schooler who had come to a boy's house when his parents weren't home, to get up to no good.

"You came," he said.

She smiled up at him. "Not yet."

He shut the front door and then wrapped his arms around her, hiking her up onto him. She laughed. "You and your theatrics."

He walked the two of them down the hallway to his room where he dropped her on the bed and climbed on top of her. "Don't ever do that again."

She just looked up at him not believing how out of control she was. She'd never felt like this before. She'd gotten wrapped up in romances with hot guys...plenty of those. But this was real. When Ryder said things, he meant them. There were no games...not anymore. This man wanted her. He wanted to be in a relationship with her. She couldn't think of anything that had thrilled or frightened her more.

He kissed her body like it was ice water in the middle of the Mojave. Her skyrocketing libido was threatening to give her a heart attack. She hadn't wanted a man like this her whole life.

Sex had functioned in different ways for her in past relationships. Sometimes she used it to hook a guy. Sometimes it was to keep a guy around who desperately needed to be gone from her life. Sometimes she used it to cure boredom.

But this was sex for the purpose of having this man close to her and inside of her in a way that she had never known until him and would never know after him.

Their clothes came off in a flurry. Meade wasn't sure who took off what of each other's. They were just trying to get to one another as quickly as possible. His cock rested against her inner thigh, and she thought she might die if he didn't enter her right that second.

"I don't think I can handle foreplay," he said between kisses. "I just want inside of you."

"Then get inside of me."

He started to roll off of her, but she grabbed him. "You can skip the condom if you want. I'm on birth control."

He considered her. "What about your always-use-a-condom rule?"

"Apparently I break all my rules with you."

He smiled, giving her a sincere kiss. He pulled away and studied her. "Has there been anyone else?"

"No."

The relief relaxed his face. "I was worried, I've got to tell you."

"You really didn't have a reason to be. Did I have a reason to worry?"

He cocked his head to the side. "I think you know me better than that." He bit his lip, rubbing his thumb over her jawline. "Meade, I—"

She shut him up with a kiss. She couldn't hear an *I love you* right now. She was way too emotional. It would do her in. "Tell me later. Just get inside me now."

He guided himself into her, and the sensation of his skin directly inside of her had her practically whimpering. She wrapped her legs around him as he moved on her, their bodies entwined and in sync. When she knew she couldn't hang on another second without coming apart, she squeezed his shoulders. "Come inside me."

I didn't take him long to follow her instructions and then he collapsed on top of her, both of them working to recover even breaths. She wanted to wrap her arms around him and hold him there all night.

He kissed her neck and then rolled off of her, positioning himself beside her on the bed. He brushed the hair off of her face and kissed her on the lips. He pulled away. "I'm so glad you're here."

"I'm glad I'm here too." Her heart wasn't showing signs of slowing. She was terrified of what came next. The games were over. It was no longer time for her to make some sassy comment and keep him guessing. Up next was a relationship. A real one. A healthy one with a great guy who would treat her like a queen. She had no idea what that looked like.

"I know I'm not supposed to be making any big sudden moves," he said, "but I don't know how to play it cool. I'm not a cool guy. When I want something, I just go for it. Having to walk this line with you has been one of the most frustrating and challenging things I've ever done in my life."

Her heart clinched. "I'm sorry I made you frustrated."

"The best things in life don't come easy, do they?" He ran his knuckles over her torso.

"Are you sure you're ready to do this with me for real?"

"There's no question for me. I know it's scary for you, but it's not for me. I know what I want. It's a whole lot scarier thinking of not having you."

She closed her eyes, shaking her head. "This is just all so weird. I'm not used to this."

"What are you used to?"

"Erratic relationships with the wrong men. Feeling desperate all the time or smothered. Right now, I just feel like I'm in the right place."

He squeezed her hip. "You're in the exact right place."

She let out a huff of air. "How do you always know the right thing to say?"

"I just say what I feel." He took her hand. "Don't sweat this. We're gonna walk through this together. Tell me what your worst fears are about a relationship with me."

She swallowed hard, looking at the ceiling, getting her bearings. "I'm afraid I'm going to do something stupid."

"Like what?"

"I don't know. You've got a fifteen-year-old daughter." She looked at him. "You know she's been texting me these past couple of weeks, right?"

"She has?"

"Yes, and I felt weird about it, but I didn't know how to handle it. It's not like I wanted to text you and tell you to have her quit texting me. But I'm also an adult and she's someone else's kid. It didn't feel right, but it felt wrong to stop."

"I'm sorry she put you in that position."

"I wasn't. She needs someone. She's going through a lot right now."

His eyebrows drew together. "Anything I need to know about?"

Meade shrugged. "I don't know. This is the kind of thing that freaks me out."

He ran his hand over her waist. "I don't mean to stress you out."

She sat up. "That's the whole thing with you. I like you, Ryder. I think you know that. But it's not just the two of us in this relationship. There are three of us. And I'm not a parent. I have no idea what I'm doing. I feel like I'm Annabella's age. That's probably why we get along so well. I've never really grown up, gotten a real job, and all that. I have, but it always falls through. I'm in no shape or position to parent a fifteen-year-old."

He sat up with her. "I understand. You're brand new to this. And Annabella is not your responsibility. She's mine."

"Exactly, and I don't want to do or say anything that hampers that. I already screwed up with the whole thing that got her in trouble at school."

"You didn't screw up. You empowered her. I can't say I'm terribly upset about it, knowing that little bastard could've helped her and didn't. Just be who you are. Don't overthink it. She's my responsibility and I try to lead her to the right places, but she's also fifteen. I am fully aware that she listens way more to her peers than she does to me. That's been the case since she was about eight years old. She makes her own decisions and she has to accept the consequences. I just have to be there to pick up the pieces when they fall."

Meade let out a sigh. "Are you going to tell her about us?"

He ran his thumb over her knee. "Are you ready for that?"

She looked him in the eye and nodded. "I am."

Relief flooded his face, and he pulled her over to him, scooting them back down on the bed. She lay in the crook of his arm with her head on his shoulder. She never felt more like she was at home than at that moment.

"I'll tell her tomorrow. I'm picking her up at ten. I'll take her out to breakfast and break the news. Honestly, I think she's going to be thrilled. She connects with you better than any woman I've ever been with or any friend I've ever seen her with."

The weight of his words bore down on her chest. She loved Annabella, but being her friend had so many landmines. "I just ask that you give me some grace as I figure my way through this."

He squeezed her to him. "We're figuring our way through it together."

Chapter Twenty-Two

A noise made Meade blink awake. A slamming door? But Ryder was lying right beside her. At the sound of another door opening and closing Meade began shaking Ryder. "Someone's in your house."

Before Ryder could respond, a voice called out, "Meade?" It was Annabella. "Dad? Why is Meade's car here? Where are y'all?"

Ryder sat up. "Just a minute." He shot up and closed the bedroom door. Meade pulled the covers up to her neck, paralyzed. This could not be happening.

Annabella went quiet, and Meade could just imagine that she was figuring it all out. She covered her eyes. "Fuck."

Ryder pulled his shorts on. "I was supposed to pick her up at ten. I don't know why she's here."

Meade jumped out of bed and found her clothes. As she dressed, she remembered a moment in high school when she had snuck into a boy's bedroom through the window and heard his mother walking down the hall at three in the morning.

Once they were both fully dressed, they just stood there looking at each other. She shrugged. "I think the cat's out of the bag."

He nodded, looking like he was accepting his fate. He ran his hand through his hair. "Are you ready for this?"

"As I'll ever be."

He opened the bedroom door.

"Should I come with you?" she asked.

"The option is escaping out that window. Which would you prefer?"

She rolled her eyes, giving him a smile and then followed him. They found Annabella in the kitchen, pouring herself a glass of orange juice. She looked up at both of them with a raised eyebrow, and then let a smile come through. "Weren't expecting me home, were you?"

"I thought I was picking you up at ten," Ryder said.

"Jaycee spent the night too, so her mom dropped me off."

Ryder checked the time on the microwave. "It's only eight o'clock."

"They had church."

"Ah," Ryder said, and Meade knew the small talk was over.

"So, this is a thing now?" Annabella asked.

Ryder glanced at Meade and she gave him a nod. He turned back to Annabella. "It is."

The grin widened Annabella's face. "It's about time. Geez. How long does it take you to land a girl, Dad?" She grabbed her phone and her glass and left the room. "As you were," she shouted, and Ryder looked at Meade. She shrugged, and then they both broke out in giggles.

When Meade got home, Felicity was curled up in the chair, scrolling through her phone. "There she is," Felicity said, giving Meade a mischievous look. "How was the sex?"

Meade dropped her keys on the table and collapsed on her bed. "Fantastic."

"And after?"

She let out a sigh. "I think I'm in a relationship. A real one."

Felicity set her phone down on her lap. "I am so damn happy for you."

"Really? You just got here and we're both single."

"Don't you worry about me. I always have a good time."

Meade knew it was partially true, but she wondered if Felicity wasn't just great at putting on a brave face. "This doesn't mean I'm going to be one of those assholes who abandons all their friends for a guy."

"Oh yes it does. We all do that, sweetie. Let's just be honest. It's okay. I'm a grown-ass woman. I know how to make friends."

"That's for sure. How did your night go?"

Felicity shrugged. "I actually just came back here. Was kind of nice having the place to myself." She lifted an eyebrow. "Does this mean you're going to surrender this wonderfully-located reasonably-priced apartment to me soon?"

"Don't get too comfortable just yet. Nobody's asked anybody to move in and nobody has agreed to such a thing."

"I hear you. But those are next steps. We both know it, especially since you don't have a house to sell or anything. You're mobile."

Meade gave her a look. "I've been that way on purpose."

"And it's finally paid off. When do you break the news to his daughter?"

Meade flopped back on the bed. "Oh, that's the fun part." She told Felicity the story.

"Wow. Scarred for life. Look at you." Felicity patted the air with her hand. "High five."

Meade shook her head and then sat up. "What a shit show. He was going to take her out to breakfast and break it to her gently."

"What's the new plan?"

"He's going to take her out to lunch and try to get a read off of her. I mean she seems happy about it. She wasn't pissed off or anything, but you know, there could be stuff there."

"There's stuff there. We all know that. But this is just what happens when you're in a relationship with a single parent."

Meade shook her head at herself. "I can't believe I've escaped that all these years and now, here I am. And it's with the one guy who I actually care about in a real way and not in some twisted, delusional way." Their phones dinged in unison and they both picked them up. "Gender reveal party," Meade said aloud. "That doesn't sound like Shayla."

"But I'll tell you who it sounds exactly like...Chase. That kid is going to have every bell and whistle known to man, even before he's born."

"Are you gonna go?" Meade asked.

"I think I'm busy that day," Felicity said, dropping her phone in her lap. Felicity met Chase at the same time Maya met Bo, and the two of them had a week-long fling that moved into a friends-with-benefits situation. When she'd come down for Maya's wedding, she stayed with Chase, which was the same weekend Chase and Shayla started their relationship. Not awkward at all.

Meade winced. "I know. But Shayla is really cool. I'm sure she's totally okay with you by now."

"Sweetie, I know Shayla is cool as they come, but I was fuck buddies with her husband up until the day they got together. And that hasn't been that long ago. I'm

171

gonna let the dust settle on this just a little longer before I come around."

"I guess it is just a gender reveal party. It's not like it's the social event of the season."

"Really? You don't think it will be, knowing Chase?" Felicity gave her a doubtful look.

"Okay, maybe it will be. But if you change your mind, we can go together."

"Or you could go with Ryder. I'm sure he's on the invite. Or he can officially be your plus one. That's what people in relationships do, you know."

Meade shook her head. "So weird."

"Yep."

Meade's phone dinged again. It was a text from Annabella.

Are you my new mommy?

Meade gave Felicity a look as she showed her the phone.

The next text was a laughing emoji followed by LMAO.

"Look at this," Meade said. "This girl has zero respect for me. How am I going to do this?"

"One day at a time, friend. One day at a time."

Chapter Twenty-Three

After a couple of weeks at the Lambert household, Meade thought she understood what a new puppy felt like. Everyone wanted to play with her, and one got jealous when the other got too much of her attention. Ryder was the adult, so he often gave in to Annabella, which was starting to take a toll on their relationship.

On the few nights Meade had off, she would hang at their house until ten o'clock. And then one night Annabella said, "For God's sake. I'm not a child. I know you two are having sex, so you might as well just do it here," which made Meade never want to have sex with Ryder again. Not really, but it was pretty weird.

They had taken to trysts at Meade's house. Ryder would drop off Annabella for school and then swing by Meade's place. Felicity would obligingly head off to a coffee shop while the two of them got it on for half an hour, always making Ryder late for work. He said he worked his own hours, but she knew this was taking a toll on him. Neither one of them liked the *wham! bam! thank you ma'am* of it. That had been exactly what Meade had tried to avoid in the beginning—sex for logistical reasons. But she had come to understand that being with a decent guy who she really liked didn't come wrapped in a perfect package.

Ryder buried his head between Meade's breasts. "I just want one night together, just the two of us."

She rubbed his back. "I know. Be patient."

"I feel terrible saying that about my own daughter. But she likes you so damn much that it's putting a kink in our love life."

"Wouldn't you say that's a good problem to have?"

"I would definitely say that." He gave her that look like he wanted to say those three little words, which still freaked her out.

"Does she babysit?" Meade asked, blurting out the first thing that came to her mind.

"She did in New Orleans, just before we left. But she hasn't since we've been here."

"My neighbors across the street have a little kid. The wife's pregnant with their second. She's been telling my next-door neighbor Sarah how desperate she is for a night out. They don't have any family around here. Sarah was telling me about it because she was feeling guilty for not volunteering."

He sat up. "Do you think you could hook them up?"

Meade laughed. "I can see. I don't really know that woman very well, but Sarah does. I can see if she'll connect her with Annabella. I think the couple is pretty desperate."

"I know the feeling," he said, giving her a significant look. He kissed her on the lips. "Hope. Thank you."

"It's not like you're not getting plenty of sex."

"It's not just the sex. It's you and me time. Every time I'm over here, we're on the clock."

"The clock will be ticking that night too. You'll have

to pick her up from babysitting sometime. And pregnant women don't stay out late."

"I could pick you up as soon as I dropped her off and take you back to my place so we don't run Felicity off."

"Or, we could go on a date?" She didn't think he was taking advantage of her, but she wanted to remind him that she was a woman in need of wooing.

He rubbed his forehead. "I'll take you on a date. I'm so sorry."

"Stop it. I'm just reminding you that there's more to dating than logistics."

"Of course there is." He got up off the bed. "I'm going to take you on the most amazing date you've ever been on. Be prepared to be wowed."

"Are you sure you want to set that kind of standard for yourself? You already pulled out all the stops on our first date."

He waved her off. "A children's museum? Please. Just you wait." He bent down, kissed her one more time, and gave her a huge smile before heading out the door.

As Ryder drove toward Meade's house, Annabella kept her head buried in her phone, a puffed up look on her face. She was ticked at him because she didn't want to babysit. It was hard for him to believe that he had raised a daughter who was, plain and simple, lazy. Ryder wasn't a lazy person. He worked and he worked out, and he cooked and cleaned the house and took care of all his daughter's stuff. But somehow, she didn't think she was responsible for doing anything. He supposed he'd always done everything for her and she probably assumed it would be that way for the rest of her life.

"You'll earn money," he said.

"Why do I need money?"

It dawned on him that he bought her everything she ever wanted. Why would she need money? He just rolled his eyes at himself as he pulled into Meade's driveway.

Meade was standing outside with a cluster of people. The neighbor who lived next-door, Sarah, stood there along with a young couple. A little boy looking around four or five years old ran around the yard in a pair of swim trunks with both of the sixteen-year-old boys who lived next-door to Meade chasing him with squirt guns.

Ryder and Annabella got out of the car and walked up to the group. They exchanged hellos and introductions, and then the mother shouted out for her young son, who promptly ignored her. One of the twin boys snatched the kid up and carried him over like a football, which appeared to delight the kid to no end. The older boy sat the young one down in front of him and held onto his shoulders like he was his dad.

"Samuel, this is Annabella. She's going to be your babysitter this evening," the boy's mom said.

"Tevin and Tanner want to be my babysitter too."

The boy's mom gave him a doubtful look. "I don't think that's true."

"They want to take me swimming in their pool."

"Maybe another time," the dad said.

"No, they're getting ready to go swimming right now. They said I could come."

The mom scratched her forehead. "Sweetie, that's not what the plan is for tonight."

Annabella shrugged. "We can go swimming."

Ryder watched a look being exchanged between Annabella and one of the boys. He couldn't tell these two kids apart, but this was probably the same one who had a crush on Meade. He knew a girl crazy teenage boy when he saw one. He once was one.

The mom and dad exchanged a look. The same boy who had been making eyes at his daughter said, "I'm a lifeguard. So is Tanner."

The mom of the older boys shrugged. "They are

certified lifeguards, and we're home. If they want to swim, it really is fine."

"Annabella doesn't have a swimsuit," Ryder said, as if this solved the problem.

"Meade probably has one I can borrow," Annabella said. Everyone in the group looked at Meade and she nodded.

The mom and dad gave each other a shrug. "It would keep them occupied," the dad said and the mom agreed.

The teenage boy picked up the little kid again. "We'll watch him while Annabella changes."

The couple exchanged some information with Annabella, said their goodbyes, and headed toward their car while Meade and Annabella went to Meade's place, leaving Ryder and the teenage boys' mom standing there awkwardly. Ryder made small talk with her until Meade and Annabella came walking back toward them. Ryder thought he was going to lose his lunch when he saw his daughter in the skimpiest bikini known to man.

"They went ahead to the pool," Sarah said, as if Ryder's daughter was just going to go back there looking like that in front of her two teenage boys.

"Cool," Annabella said as she trotted off.

Ryder took a step toward her, but Meade blocked his way. "You ready?"

Ryder blinked himself back to reality. Meade raised her eyebrows at him.

"Don't worry," Sarah said. "The boys are lifeguards. I told them they should offer to babysit, but neither one of them would. I don't know why teenage kids these days are so lazy."

On a better day, Ryder could probably have a good long conversation with this woman, but right now, all he could think about was those two horny teenage boys looking at his daughter in that bikini.

Sarah said her goodbyes, leaving Meade and Ryder

standing on the driveway. "Are you okay?" Meade asked.

"Yeah," Ryder said, feeling completely out of sorts.

"Do you still want to go?"

"Of course. He opened the car door for Meade and walked around the front, trying to get a glimpse of his daughter at the pool. She was stepping down the stairs while the kid splashed around and both boys jumped in the pool.

The toot of the car horn got his attention, and he opened the door, getting into the car.

"Are you really worried about this? The boys are lifeguards. I'm sure it will be fine. The kid's parents were even okay with it."

"It's not the kid I'm worried about."

"Is this about Annabella?"

He just gave Meade a look and strapped himself in. "Did you see the way that one kid was looking at her?"

"No."

"Did you not have a one-piece?" As soon as he said it, he knew it was over the line.

"Do I seem like someone who would have a one-piece bathing suit to you?"

Ryder just pursed his lips and backed out of the driveway.

"These boys' parents are right there. What do you think they're going to do?" she asked.

"I just don't like the way that one kid was looking at her."

"Like he thought she was cute? Ryder, she's getting ready to be sixteen. She's going to start dating. She probably already has been."

He jerked his head toward her. "What do you mean?"

"Do you think this is the first time she's ever talked to a boy?"

"Of course not. But maybe it's the first time in a bikini like that."

Meade turned her whole body toward him, and he knew he was in for it. "I can't believe you're acting this way. This is a totally innocent situation. Nobody has done anything wrong. Parents are involved. Everyone has approved except you."

"That's because I'm the one with the teenage daughter who just got humiliated by a little teenage prick."

"Tanner and Tevin are good guys."

"Oh, because you know them so well?"

Meade just stared at him and then finally said, "Do you just want to take me back home?"

"No. I'm sorry. It's just that something happened with that other kid a few weeks ago and now this. I'm not ready for her to start dating."

"Well, you need to get ready because it's happening whether you want it to or not."

"What do you know?"

"Ryder, don't put me in this position."

"Has she been dating?"

Meade just shook her head and looked out the window.

They rode in silence to the restaurant, which gave Ryder the opportunity to review his behavior and realize what a jackass he'd been. He pulled into a parking space and turned to her. "I'm sorry. I don't know what got into me."

"You're a protective father. There's no apology necessary."

"There is. I shouldn't have indicated that you gave her an inappropriate bathing suit."

"Don't worry about it. Like I say, I don't know what I'm doing. That's just the bathing suit I had and what I wear. I'm not fifteen."

"But fifteen-year-old girls do wear bathing suits like that," he admitted, however reluctantly.

She shrugged. "This is a really nice restaurant. Let's just go in and enjoy it."

"Absolutely."

Chapter Twenty-Four

The date was everything Ryder had promised. The restaurant had a table like no other on 30A…in Florida maybe. They were seated at a private captain's lookout with an open view of the Gulf of Mexico, the waves lapping up to the shore. The wine was amazing and really expensive. The food was delicious and the courses were plentiful. All was to spec except for one thing. Ryder was not there with her. He was back on her street standing over his daughter and making sure nothing happened, or at least he was in his mind.

After Ryder paid the bill, Meade squeezed his hand. "Thank you. This really was incredible."

"Yeah, the food was good."

"We could go for a walk on the beach. Nobody's down there right now since it's dark. It'll be just us and the ghost crabs."

He checked the time on his phone. "Maybe we should get back."

"I gave Annabella a key to my place. I told her she

could go there if they got home before we got back."

He rubbed his head with his thumb and forefinger. "Yeah, okay."

Meade gave him a doubtful look. "Or we can go back to my place."

He met her gaze. "I'm sorry. I'm obsessing, I know."

"Has she never been out on an official date?"

"Not that I'm aware of. No kid has come to our house to pick her up. I knew we were getting to that point, but I just didn't know it was tonight."

"It's not tonight. She's babysitting tonight."

He looked up at her with wide eyes. "You don't think she would take one of those boys to your place with her, do you?"

Meade let the tension out of her shoulders. "No, I do not think she would do that."

Ryder bit his lip, the look of worry consuming his face.

Meade slid her chair back. "Let's go to my place."

"Would you mind?"

"I wouldn't. But I would ask myself this question if I were you. Have you talked to her about birth control?"

"What?" he asked with a look of panic flooding his face.

"I'm not saying she needs it tonight. But if you're this worried, you need to ask yourself exactly what you're worried about and then take steps to prevent whatever that is if you can. Talking to her about sex and her options with birth control and condoms would be one of those steps."

"Why would I want to offer that? That's just an open invitation."

"Or insurance that she doesn't end up with a baby just like you did."

They walked in silence to the car and he let her in. As they drove back to Meade's place, she knew she had dropped a bomb on him. But as much as she hated to admit it, she was starting to get concerned about

Annabella as well. Annabella did a lot of things based on emotion. She wasn't a leader of the pack. She was a follower.

Meade knew because she was just like her when she was that age. Annabella would become a leader, but it wasn't going to happen tonight or this month or maybe even this year. Meade could talk to Annabella all day long about having self-confidence and sticking to what she wants for herself. But Annabella was erratic in her decisions. Anything could happen at any time.

When they got back to Meade's place, Ryder peered around the back of Sarah's house at the pool, but of course everyone was gone from there. "Should we go check on her across the street?" he asked.

"No, we should not. You could text her though."

Ryder took out his phone and thumbed into it. "You don't think one of those boys is over there with her, do you?"

"I think we need to go inside my place and wait patiently. I can even think of some things we could do while we wait." She put her hand on her hip and cocked her head to the side.

He followed Meade to the house, but she knew she wasn't getting any that evening.

She sat next to him on the bed, squeezing his thigh. "Any chance I can have you here with me, just for a moment?"

He gave her a weak smile. "I'm sorry I ruined our night."

"Our night is still going. There's a chance for you to redeem yourself."

He just looked at her with a stressed-out expression on his face. She settled in at the top of the bed with her back on the headboard. "Come over here and we'll watch a show on my phone while we wait."

"I'm sorry. I'm going to make this up to you big time."

"Oh yeah you will," she said as she pulled up a video she'd been wanting to check out on space plasma. It wasn't like he was going to be paying attention to what they were watching anyway.

They had moved into a video on interstellar ice processes when a knock sounded at the door. Ryder jumped up like they were under a fire drill and opened the door. Annabella stood there, and Ryder's shoulders visibly dropped in relief. "They're home?"

"Yep. And I'm forty bucks richer."

Meade chuckled. "When I was babysitting, I counted myself lucky if I got five dollars an hour."

"That was seriously the easiest money I've ever earned. I told them to let me know anytime they want to go out. And they liked it so much that they said they were going to start doing it every Saturday night."

Ryder scratched his forehead. "Won't that interfere with your social schedule?"

"For this kind of money, who cares?"

"You've lost her, Ryder," Meade said. "She's learning the concept of capitalism."

Annabella pulled a plastic bag out of her purse. "Here's your bathing suit. I can wash it for you."

"No, it's fine. I'll just wash it out in the sink."

"Thanks for letting me borrow it."

"How did it go at the pool?" Ryder asked.

"It was good. Samuel loves swimming. We seriously had to drag him out of the pool when it started getting dark. Are we heading out, or are we hanging for a while?"

"We can go." Ryder turned to Meade with a look of exhaustion on his face like she had never seen. "Thank you for putting up with me tonight."

"I had a good time," she lied.

"Why don't you come back with us," Annabella suggested.

Meade checked her phone. "It's already ten-thirty."

"So. Just stay the night. It's not that big of a deal. Seriously, you two are being so weird about this. Just stay the night."

Ryder and Meade exchanged a look, and Meade said, "Maybe another night."

Ryder handed Annabella the keys. "Why don't you wait in the car." Annabella shrugged and headed out.

Ryder collapsed on the bed. "I really don't want to end the night this way."

Meade just tossed up a hand, not knowing what else to say or do.

"I want you to come home with us," he said, but by the look on his face, it wasn't really a clear invitation.

"That's up to you."

He just looked at her like he was hoping the answers would fall out of the sky. "You know, you're not the only one who doesn't know what they're doing."

She chuckled, his words making her feel like less of a disaster.

"Would you be comfortable coming over?" he asked.

"How have you handled this in the past? Did women come over?"

"Not this soon. I didn't even introduce Annabella until several months into my relationships before. Most of the women I've been in relationships with never even saw my bed. I mean, I saw theirs, but you know..."

"I do. Don't need the details."

He ran his hand through his hair. "Just pack a bag and let's go."

She lifted her eyebrows. "Are you sure?"

"I'm sure. I can bring you back here on my way to work."

She stood. "Okay."

"You know," he said, sliding his hand around her waist, "you really are different. Everything is different with you. It feels like it's all unchartered territory."

She gave him a genuine smile. "It feels the same way to me."

He kissed her and then smacked her ass. "Grab your stuff so we can get home."

Meade tried not to interpret too much from his turn of phrase. It was his home, not hers. She understood that. But the way he said it like it was hers as well had been logged in her brain.

Chapter Twenty-Five

From where Ryder sat on his bed, he had a view of Meade standing in front of his bathroom mirror in her bra and panties, combing out her hair. It was hard for him to believe they were at this place in their relationship. Things hadn't been all hearts and roses since they had decided to do this thing for real, but his feelings for Meade grew stronger every day...every moment if he was being honest.

He'd been in several relationships in his adult life, but his feelings had never been this deep before. The other relationships seemed forced, now that he looked back on them. Maybe it was the Annabella factor. Maybe he'd held himself back from other women since she'd never really connected with them. But Annabella adored Meade, and so there was nothing holding him back from his feelings for her, which were growing stronger than he could contain in words.

He'd almost said those three little words to her several times, but she wasn't ready to hear them. It was like she knew each time he was getting ready to say them so she would kiss him or change the subject. He had to be careful, but he was bursting at the seams.

She was still working at the bar, which he was not wild about. He knew men hit on her all the time. For whatever reason, that bar seemed to be populated with people of their generation. It was definitely a locals' bar with the occasional tourist. But for the most part, no matter who was there, he knew they were looking at his girl. Sure, he sounded like a Neanderthal, but that's how he felt around her. He wanted to make her his permanently, but it was entirely too soon for that. He definitely had his sights set on her being with him long-term, whatever that meant for her.

She set her comb down and turned to meet his gaze. A smile crawled across her face as she strolled toward him. She straddled him, wrapping her arms around his neck. "You know we've got the house to ourselves tonight."

He knew. He almost jumped for joy when Annabella asked if she could spend the night with her friend. "Anything in particular you want to do after the party?" They were headed to Chase and Shayla's gender reveal party—their first official appearance as a couple in this group of friends.

She ground herself against him, causing his cock to twitch. "More things than I can count." She kissed him, and if she didn't stop, he was going to get past the point of no return.

He pulled away. "Are you sure we have to go?"

She cocked her head to the side. "Your daughter's still here. We've got to drop her on the way."

"I know. But we can just come back here if you want."

She stood up, pursing her lips. "Be a good boy." Her sexy voice just about did him in. He was so over the top for her.

She was telling him a story about how Shayla had called Felicity and personally asked her to come to the party after Felicity had declined the invite, when her phone buzzed from its position on the nightstand. Even though she seemed unconcerned, he was curious to know who it was. He wasn't being jealous, or at least that's what he kept telling himself. But he couldn't help his interest.

"Do you want me to bring you your phone?" he asked, hoping she'd say yes just so he could see who it was.

"Is it Maya?"

He picked up the phone and the notification on the screen had him chuckling. "No, it's Andrew Harrington. Since when do you buddy up with billionaires?" Andrew Harrington was one of the top five richest guys in the world, so clearly this was a joke—someone who was in her address book with that nickname. Maybe it was some rich ex of hers. Now his stomach was going sour. What did this asshole want? Her silence made him nervous.

She set down her makeup brush and walked over to her phone. She read the message and then put the phone face down on the nightstand.

"Do you want some privacy?" he asked, trying not to grit his teeth.

"No," she said, her face coloring.

"If it's an ex of yours, I can take it. Talk to him. See what he wants. And tell him not to text you anymore because you're with a hot marine biologist now." When she didn't laugh at his joke, he got even more worried. "Hey," he said, standing up off the bed. "Is this guy someone I should worry about?"

She let out a sigh of exhaustion like she'd run a marathon. "It's not an ex."

"Okay, then who is this guy with the same name as one of the richest guys in the world?"

She just opened her mouth and then pressed her tongue against her bottom teeth like she did when she was nervous. She tossed up a hand, rolling her eyes. "It's him. It's Andrew Harrington. It's just not a big deal so let's drop it, okay?"

He stood there dumbfounded, not understanding what she was saying. "What are you talking about?"

She went back to her makeup, patting a tiny brush into a compact. "It's him. But seriously, it's nothing. I would prefer if we could drop it and move on."

Ryder's heartbeat amped up. "Andrew Harrington is calling you for real?" It sounded ludicrous coming off his tongue, but of all the things Meade was, a liar was not one of them.

She set the makeup down and rested against the bathroom sink. "Do you remember me telling you about that thesis paper I wrote that got me that job?"

"Of course."

"Andrew found it and read it, and he asked if I would come to work for him. I said no."

Ryder put his palm to his forehead, pacing around the room. "I can't believe this. How have you not told me this already?"

"Because I'm not doing it. I don't want to do it."

He walked over to her and took her by both shoulders. "Meade, why don't you want to do it?"

"I was considering it, but Felicity helped me see that I was yet again going to go for some job that I wouldn't stay at longer than a few months and completely ruin what I have with you."

He blinked, unable to believe Felicity would dispense such ludicrous advice, even though he didn't know her. "Felicity knew that Andrew Harrington asked you to come to work for him and talked you out of it?"

"She didn't know it was Andrew Harrington. She thought it was just another job. But that doesn't matter. She was right."

Ryder went over to get Meade's phone, disappointed that the notification was gone from the screen now, and of course, it was locked.

He handed it to her. "Call this man back."

"No," she said with a frown on her face that let him know he'd crossed the line.

"I'm sorry. I didn't mean it that way." He set the phone down and collected himself. "What is the job?"

She told him about it and he thought he might lose his lunch from nerves. "Do you mean to tell me that you can play a part in people traveling to space, and you're not taking it?"

"I think it's stupid. This money should go to people who need food, not to fill some billionaire's urge to take a taxi to the moon."

Ryder couldn't argue that point so he just took a deep breath.

"Listen," Meade said, "I don't want to talk about this right now. We're getting ready to go to the gender reveal party, and I don't want this getting around. Nobody knows about this...well, except Sebastian. But he's like a bank vault. I hadn't planned on telling anybody else about it. I thought Andrew had moved on. It's been weeks since I turned him down."

Ryder just sat on the bed, nodding, unable to look at her. With her working at a bar and dressing so casually, and being willing to spend so much time with him, from time to time he forgot who she was. Sure, she'd become better about letting him watch brainy documentaries with her, but he was realizing for the first time the magnitude of her intelligence. She was someone who could change the world, literally. And he was the one holding her back from that.

Ryder was half in and half out of the conversation with Bo, Blake, and Sebastian as he watched Meade across the swimming pool in Chase and Shayla O'Neil's backyard. She was smiling and laughing at something Ashe and his boyfriend Ethan were saying to her. She glanced over at

191

Ryder and gave him an even bigger smile, holding up her drink to him in a toast. He tipped his bottle toward her then she went back to her conversation with the two men.

As crazy as he was about her, he couldn't understand any part of what she was doing. She loved astrophysics and she had the chance to take her dream job. But she was throwing it away for him. She was serving thirty-something rednecks in a Panama City Beach bar instead of sending people to outer space. Every time he thought of the enormity of that injustice, it felt like a bag of dirt was being poured over his head.

How could he enable this decision? He was complicit now. He was actively holding her back. She said she had told the guy a few weeks ago, but he was still texting. He wanted Meade. He wanted her brain. For all Ryder knew, he wanted more than that, but he had to assume this was just a work thing. The guy was famously crazy about his wife, but it's not like that meant anything.

Felicity stood with a woman who looked a little older than them whom Ryder hadn't met yet. He excused himself from the group and walked over to Felicity. She smiled as he approached, welcoming him into their conversation. "Ryder with a Y. Have you met Cassidy?"

The woman offered a hand. "You're Desiree's friend, aren't you?"

"And now he's Meade's friend too," Felicity said with a raised eyebrow.

"Ah," Cassidy said with a knowing smile. "Nice catch." Ryder shook hands with the lady who had one of the kindest smiles he'd ever seen. A guy a bit younger than all of them stepped up to her and slid his arm around her waist possessively. "Jesse, this is Ryder. He's Desiree's friend from New Orleans, and apparently now he's Meade's friend too."

"Maya's sister, right?" Jesse asked.

"Yep," Cassidy said.

"I'm getting good at this name thing." The guy shook Ryder's hand with a strong grip. "Nice to meet you, man. Meade's cool. One night we were all on the beach and she and I got talking about the stars. She showed me some cool constellations."

Ryder's stomach sank even further. "Yeah, she's interested in astronomy."

"That's awesome. How long have you been together?"

"Just a few weeks."

"Ah, early stages." He brought Cassidy even closer to him. "We're still early days as well. But I've already got her nailed down," he said, taking her left hand which had a ring on it, and kissing her hand as he met her gaze.

Seeing this couple so obviously in love and headed down the aisle gave him conflicting emotions. Part of him felt like he was right there where they were. If he continued things with Meade just as they were going now, he was headed in this direction, which made him practically giddy. On the other hand, he couldn't head down that road knowing he was holding her back from her dream.

"Chase wanted me to tell y'all that the food's ready," Jesse said.

"Oh good," Felicity said, starting to walk toward the house. "I'm starving."

Ryder followed her, taking her arm. "Actually, can I talk to you a second?"

Her eyes went wide. "Sure." They stopped and she gave him her full attention.

"Did you know that the job Meade was going to take in Texas was with Andrew Harrington?"

Felicity blinked, her jaw dropping, and then she closed her eyes and shook her head. "Of course it is. I should've known. That girl. I forget who I'm talking to most of the time. She's just so damn down to earth."

He glanced at Meade across the pool. She was still

engrossed in her conversation with the two men. "I don't know what to do. I can't just let this go."

"Or you could," Felicity said.

He looked her in the eye. "She said that you were instrumental in her decision."

"You know that's a lie. She didn't give me all the facts. If she would've wanted my real opinion, she would've told me who the job was with. All I knew was it was some job in Texas. And I also know that she's nuts about you, and you're legit. You're not some guy who's going to treat her like crap. That's something to stay around for."

Ryder ran his hand through his hair, glancing at Meade again. This time she was looking back at him and giving him a smile like he was the only guy on the planet. His heart was crushed like it'd been hit by a cinderblock. "You wouldn't think I was selfish if I stayed with her?"

"I think you'd be an idiot if you left her, but that's just my opinion."

She started to walk away, but he tapped her on the arm again and she turned to him. "If you had known the job was with Andrew Harrington, would you still have nudged her in my direction?"

Felicity thought about it. "Possibly. You're what she wants right now."

"But don't you think she really wants that job, but she's just afraid?"

"I think Meade's a big girl and is capable of making her own decisions. She made this one on her own. It's not yours to make. It's hers. You're not holding her back. You're holding her close. There's a big difference." Felicity walked away, leaving him even more confused than before.

Chapter Twenty-Six

Ryder was being weird. It was that damn Andrew Harrington. That fucker would not go away. Meade was going to have to change her phone number. And now she was risking a long, drawn-out conversation in place of the hot sex she'd been doing without lately. Even though she'd been spending the night, they'd been too uncomfortable to do anything with Annabella there, so they'd been doing a lot of cuddling and the occasional heavy petting. They'd been having way more sex when they weren't spending the night together.

Meade was doing her best to ignore his strange behavior. She was acting as if the worried expressions and lengthy stares across the yard at Chase and Shayla's house were all normal, hoping the weirdness would go away. In the car on the way home, she had stayed chatty about stuff from the party—nothing of any importance. She didn't want him asking any questions about Andrew Harrington.

They were in the bedroom taking off their clothes from the party, but rather than watching her undress, Ryder had this stressed out look on his face. She stripped down to her bra and panties and walked over to him, sliding her hands around his waist and then down south. But before she could touch him, he stopped her with his hand, turned around, and met her gaze. "Do you care if we talk for a minute first?"

She slumped, knowing she had been beat. "Can we please just not."

"Meade, you dropped a bomb on me tonight. This is important stuff. We can't just sweep this under the rug like it's not happening."

"What's not happening is us getting in this bed together naked."

"This is your dream. This is the thing that you audit classes over and write thesis papers on that you don't even get credit for. You've got to think that this is an amazing opportunity."

"What if I don't want to take the opportunity?"

"But you love space. All those videos—"

"I knew I shouldn't have shared that side of me with you."

He turned her around to face him, holding her by the shoulders. "Of course you should have. If we're gonna do this thing for real, I want to share all that kind of stuff with you."

She considered this wonderful man who only had her best interest at heart. "You know I've never shared that side of me with anyone. And there's a reason. I like to keep it private, just for myself."

"Okay, I can try to understand that."

"But you won't. What if I just want it to be something I enjoy? What if I don't want it to be my career? And don't give me that bullshit about if you love what you do you'll never work a day in your life. Space is fun to me. It's not work. I've told you before how this goes. I don't like the competition. I don't like the stress of people judging me all the time. Nobody judges me at the bar."

"They might not be judging you, but they're definitely interested in you."

"Oh God, Ryder. Please tell me you're not jealous of a bunch of rednecks?"

"Maybe I am. Is that your long-term plan? Working at that bar?"

She tossed up her hands. "I don't know what my long-term plan is. Don't you understand this about me by now? If you're in this, you need to understand that this is who I am. I don't commit to things. I work at bars or at casinos or I wait tables. I do what I feel like doing. And there's no long-term plan. If you're interested in me for real, this is something you have to accept."

He stared at her for a long time. "It's just hard when I know how much potential you have."

She turned around and walked away from him. "You sound exactly like my sister." When he didn't respond, she turned around and found him sitting on the bed. "I don't want to be stressful to you like your sister is."

"Then quit trying to fix my life. I don't want that job. I want to be right here with you, right now."

"Yeah," he said standing up. "But what about next week? Or next month?"

She shook her head at him. "I don't know about that. I just know about this."

"Did you ever stop to think that maybe I'm concerned about all this because I don't know where it leaves me?"

The tension dropped out of her shoulders. She ran her knuckles over his jawline, realizing how much this man really meant to her. "I hear you. I just don't have an answer right now. What I can say is that I want to be here. I can also tell you that I've never had this kind of relationship before. I haven't freaking been this happy before. In all my past relationships, I was on edge and stressed all the time. Somehow with you, I get that excited, nervous, giddy feeling along with the security. I didn't know that was possible."

He smiled at her, shaking his head as he gazed into her eyes. "God, I love you so much."

She froze, wondering if he meant to say that.

"I'm sorry if that makes you feel uncomfortable or trapped or like you just want to bolt out of here right this minute. But I can't keep it in any longer. I've had the words on the tip of my tongue for a while now. They can only stay locked up so long."

She bit the inside of her cheek, wanting to repeat the words back to him, but she couldn't. She had to stay strong and keep her wall up, because she knew herself, and she knew she could wake up tomorrow and be ready to flee. Or she could fuck something up royally and have to flee.

He pulled her to him. "I love you." He kissed her and then pulled away. "I just needed you to know it."

He walked her to the bed and unhooked her bra. She stepped out of her panties and lay back on the bed as he pulled down his boxers. He climbed on top of her and kissed every inch of her body from her neck to her knees, making up for all the quickies from the past few weeks. When he got to her core, she sucked in a breath and then let herself relax, allowing him to love her, because that was the only way to describe what he was doing to her right then, loving every inch of her.

Chapter Twenty-Seven

Ryder had passed the test. He had told Meade that he loved her and she hadn't slipped out of his bedroom in the middle of the night, never to be heard from again. Instead, they'd made love a number of times, and then she'd fallen asleep in his arms. He had woken up with her hand gripping his cock, which could not possibly have been a better alarm clock. Now they were in the kitchen making breakfast together, him on the griddle with French toast and her cutting up a cantaloupe.

They'd picked up Annabella early since the family she stayed with had church, so his daughter was sitting on the couch with her face and thumbs engrossed in her phone as usual.

"Out of curiosity," Ryder said, "what did that guy want when he texted you yesterday?"

She grabbed the pineapple and turned it on its side on the cutting board. "He's coming to town with his family on vacation. He asked if he could take me out to dinner. He wants me to meet his wife."

Ryder was trying not to be starstruck, but it was difficult. "Wow. That sounds like a big honor. His wife is famously private."

"Whatever. It's just another tactic."

"Do you think he planned his vacation here just so he could take you out?"

"I'm not so vain to believe that."

"I'm serious. Wouldn't a guy like that vacation in Turks and Caicos or Fiji?"

"I don't know where people vacation."

He glanced into the living room at his daughter and then scooted toward Meade. "Annabella is a huge fan of his daughter. If you want to tell her this, it would solidify your spot in the Cool Hall of Fame."

Meade squinted at him and then said, "Oh yeah, she's like an influencer or something, isn't she?"

"Ask Annabella. She'll tell you all about it."

Meade chopped for a while in silence. "He said I could bring my family."

Ryder tried not to get too excited. He had to play it cool. "Are you thinking about Maya?"

She cut her eyes at him with a smile. "I think you know who I'm thinking about."

"You would certainly win points with Annabella."

"I don't need to win any points with Annabella."

"True. But it would solidify you as her favorite adult on the planet. How's that?"

"I'm pretty sure you are her favorite adult on the planet."

He pointed his spatula at her. "Do not take that to the bank."

They finished making breakfast, bumping up against one another when they could, and pretty much acting like crazy teenagers in love. He knew he was one, and he suspected she was getting there too. He just had to keep walking the line between loving her like crazy and scaring her off.

He called Annabella to the table, and she walked in zombie-like, face still planted in the phone. He held his hand out for her phone.

"I thought that was only during dinnertime," she said.

"We've made a pretty elaborate breakfast here. We'd like to see your face while we eat it together."

She rolled her eyes and handed it to him. He tucked it away in a drawer and then they all sat down together.

While Annabella was forking a piece of French toast, Ryder nudged Meade under the table and nodded toward Annabella.

Meade rolled her eyes at him but she had a proud smile on her face, nonetheless. "I hear you're a fan of Aspen Harrington."

"Oh my God," Annabella said, picking up the bowl of fruit. "She is amazing. She does these videos where she sits down with different celebrities and they do something stupid like shuffle cups or flip bottles but it's awesome. They end up talking to her about stuff. She has this way of like digging into their souls. It's the coolest thing ever."

"Mmm," Meade uttered, playing it cool.

"Why? Where did that come from?" Annabella asked.

"Oh, no reason. I just wondered if maybe you'd like to meet her."

Annabella froze, staring at Meade. She finally looked over at Ryder. "What is she talking about?"

He couldn't help himself. "Meade has connections. She's been invited to dinner with the Harringtons and she can bring guests."

Annabella stood up, almost knocking the whole table over. "Shut up. You're not serious."

Meade let out a giggle. "I am serious. I should've told you before breakfast so I didn't end up wearing mine all over me."

"Is this for real? You two aren't playing some stupid

joke? Because if you are, it's not funny."

"Just sit down and I'll tell you all about it," Meade said.

Ryder cleaned up from breakfast while Meade stood outside on the deck talking with Andrew Harrington. It was going to take him a while to get used to that. The man had enough money to buy and sell the United States, and he was talking to the love of Ryder's life. Surreal didn't begin to cover it.

She came back inside, shutting the French doors and then pocketing her phone. She made her way to the kitchen. "Sorry I didn't help. I didn't think it would take that long."

"Well?" he asked.

"We're all set for tomorrow night."

He tossed a wet paper towel into the trashcan. "So, this is happening, huh?"

"I guess."

Annabella came running into the kitchen. "And Aspen will be there?"

"He said she would be. I can't make any guarantees though."

"We've got to go shopping. I can't wear anything in my closet." Annabella said.

Meade shrugged at Ryder. "I can take her shopping."

"Do you guys want some girl time?"

Annabella considered him. "You can come if you want, but don't try to hurry us."

"I wouldn't dream of it. I will be the picture of patience."

"We'll hold you to that," Meade said, bumping him with her hip. "I'll go put my shopping shoes on."

As they settled into a table in the open-air seating of the outdoor mall, shopping bags on either side of him, Ryder could not remember ever feeling more like he had a family. There was always a stressful vibe between other women he dated and his daughter, even on good days. But Meade and Annabella were like two peas in a pod. They just got each other somehow. If Ryder didn't want Meade so much for himself, he would wish she was a fifteen-year-old girl so she could be Annabella's best friend.

After they ordered, he checked his email, which he had been ignoring all day. Even though it was Saturday, his work never stopped.

He frowned. "Annabella, what do you have going on at school on Thursday and Friday?"

"I don't know, why?"

"I've got to go down to Sarasota again."

Annabella let out an irritated grunt. "Not again. Last time I was stuck in the hotel room the whole time."

"I can't help it. I can talk to your teachers again."

"You take her with you when you go out of town for work?" Meade asked.

He shrugged. "I don't really have another option. It usually has worked out okay with school. Teachers will give her the work ahead of time, reschedule a test if there happens to be one. They usually work with me."

"I'll stay with her."

"You don't need to do that," he said.

"Dad, yes, let Meade come over and stay with me. That would be perfect. I don't need to miss school, anyway. I'm getting too old for this."

Ryder pursed his lips at his daughter. "You weren't too old for it last semester."

"Seriously, Dad. I have school. You don't need to be plucking me out like I'm in second grade. I've got important stuff going on."

He considered her. "I know. It's just that…" He really had no excuse. And if he and Meade were going to do this together, he needed to show that he trusted her.

"I really don't mind," Meade said. "We'll have a good time together. It'll give us some girl time."

"What was today?" Ryder asked.

"Interrupted girl time," Annabella said.

Ryder rolled his eyes with a smile. "Okay. Only if you're sure you don't mind."

"I don't mind," Meade said, squeezing his knee under the table.

And then his two girls launched into a conversation about kids at Annabella's school who Ryder had never heard of before. But Meade nodded along as if it all made perfect sense.

Ryder just sat back and watched his whole world right in front of him at the table. He had to swallow down a lump in his throat. He'd never been so happy.

Chapter Twenty-Eight

When Ryder pulled up in the parking lot of the Italian restaurant on 30A that Meade had chosen for their dinner with Andrew Harrington, he shouldn't have been surprised to see a series of brand new, luxury package, black SUVs with tinted windows, and only a few other cars there. He couldn't help himself. "Is the President of the United States in town?"

Meade just stared at the cars with her eyebrows drawn together. Was she starting to get a little nervous?

He parked the car, and they all got out. As they approached the door, he noticed a sign that read, CLOSED FOR PRIVATE PARTY.

"I didn't even think to check for..." Meade trailed off as Ryder lifted his eyebrows.

"What?" Annabella asked.

Meade rolled her eyes. "We are the private party."

Annabella beamed. "Cool."

As they walked into the restaurant, a woman dressed in business casual approached them with a wide smile.

"Meade. It's so nice to meet you." She held out her hand and Meade shook it. "I'm Whitney. I work for Andrew." She acknowledged both Annabella and Ryder by name, and then said, "Andrew and the family are in the back room. You can follow me."

"We have the place to ourselves?" Meade asked, glancing around at the handful of people gathered here and there, each giving them a nod and a smile as they passed.

"They are all with us. Andrew travels with a handful of staff. As you know, he has four kids. We've found it's better just to rent a restaurant out to accommodate the family, and the staff usually comes along since we have the whole place to ourselves." She shrugged as if to say, *Why not.*

Ryder gave Meade a look, but she was too busy viewing her surroundings with an expression on her face as if she felt like she was in Siberia.

In the next section of the restaurant Andrew Harrington was busy coloring on a paper placemat with a child next to him who looked about four or five years old. The thought passed through Ryder's mind that it could all be a set up so that he could sell Meade on what a big family guy he was. But the way the man and his wife were interacting with the kids didn't seem fake.

His wife spotted them first and nudged her husband, who turned to them and beamed like he had won the lottery. The man already had all the money in the world, so in this case, the lottery was Meade. Ryder had encouraged this dinner, but now he couldn't help regretting it. What if Andrew was successful in winning her over tonight? Ryder loved Meade and wanted the best things for her, including this job if that was the right thing. But it felt very wrong to him.

"Meade Forbes in the flesh." Andrew Harrington walked over and held out his hand to her, gazing at her like she was a rock star. "I was beginning to wonder if I would ever be able to meet you in person."

Meade's face colored, causing Ryder's stomach to go nervous. But he couldn't blame her for being starstruck. He would be if he wasn't on the defense. This man wanted to take the love of his life from him. "This is Ryder and his daughter, Annabella," Meade said.

As they exchanged greetings, the wife joined them. "Thank you for indulging us. We really appreciate you making the time. I'm Jenny. Please, come and sit with us."

Several tables had been pushed together to make one long, rectangular table. A girl looking close to Annabella's age sat in the spot next to the first of three empty chairs on one side, and Ryder wondered if this was the famous Aspen. Annabella seemed to have frozen in her spot, but Meade nudged her toward the empty chair next to the girl. "Why don't you sit here," Meade said, encouraging her toward the seat. The young girl stood, a smile brightening her face. "It's Annabella, right? I'm Aspen."

"I'm Annabella, but you just said that." She giggled with an eye roll.

They all sat, and after a complicated ordering process that involved many different food allergies and preferences, all the kids jumped up from the table and were led out of the room by one of Andrew's people. Aspen asked Annabella if she'd like to take a walk, and the four adults were left alone.

Jenny folded her hands together, setting her elbows on the table, focusing on Meade. "So, I have got to fangirl just a little bit. The section in your paper about magnetohydrodynamics left me speechless." She leaned in. "And I've been dying to talk to you about black holes." The woman's eyes got wide like she was revealing government secrets about aliens.

"You'll have to forgive her," Andrew said. "She's a

complete geek." His wife nudged him playfully, and he smiled back at her like a man who had a great life.

"You study Astrophysics?" Meade asked Jenny.

"How do you think I got into it?" Andrew said with his arm on the back of his wife's chair.

The two women launched into a conversation that Ryder had a hard time following.

"Want to check out the bar? We have it all to ourselves," Andrew said to Ryder.

He looked at Meade and she nodded, turning her attention back to Jenny. Ryder followed Andrew, who had the gait of someone who owned the place. Ryder supposed he did, at least for the evening.

A bartender who had been looking at his phone set it down and took their drink orders. Ryder turned to Andrew. "So, your wife is the astrophysicist in the family?"

"Yep. But she's like Meade. It wasn't her primary field of study in college."

"I figured the world would know if it had been," Ryder said.

"Jenny's private. She'd never have her picture taken again if it were up to her."

"And you?"

The man shrugged. "I don't mind the spotlight, as I'm sure you can tell," he said with an arrogant grin that Ryder wasn't sure if he respected or wanted to slap off his face.

"Are we here because you want Meade or because your wife wants her?"

"My wife found her. I'll admit to that. She's very supportive of women in the field, so I'm not sure I would've known about the paper without Jenny. But after I read it, there was no question that Meade was coming to work for me."

Ryder's chest burned. Even though he had been encouraging Meade to go work for this guy, he didn't like this asshole making definitive statements about her one way or the other. "I think that's up to her, don't you?"

"She's definitely turned me down more times than any woman has in my life. That's a blow to the ego, I'll admit." The bartender handed them their drinks, and Andrew took a sip of his whiskey and then set it down and met Ryder's gaze. "But that woman cannot be wasted in Panama City serving drinks to local rednecks."

Ryder became suddenly protective of the people of this area. "Don't you think it's a little elitist of you to be calling the hard-working people of this area rednecks?"

Andrew waved him off. "I'm a little red myself. I'm from Texas. I've never made any bones about that. But that's neither here nor there. What I want to know is if you love her, how can you hold her down here?"

Ryder's heart rate increased. "You must not know Meade very well. She makes her own decisions."

"Of course she does. Do you think I would want her to come work for me if she wasn't a strong-willed woman? What I want to know is why you won't encourage her to go?"

"Why do you think we're here tonight?"

"She told me you were the one who talked her into this. But if there's one thing I do when I want something, it's research. I know Meade's background. I know where she's worked and I know where she's lived. And I know how long she holds down jobs. I also know if she can find any excuse to get out of this, she will. But I want her, and more importantly, my wife wants her. So, she will be coming to Texas to work for us. You can encourage that and make this an easy transition, or we can all do this the hard way."

Ryder's blood was red hot. "Are you seriously sitting here threatening me?"

"Not at all. I'm just telling you it's going to happen. And you know it needs to happen. This is an opportunity of a lifetime for her. She and my wife will geek out on all the space stuff. They'll be like pigs in slop."

Ryder could not believe this man's analogy. As he was trying to find his next words, Andrew squinted at him. "Don't get all high and mighty on me. It's a Texas saying. My point is, you know this is what she wants and you know it's what she needs. And I know the two of you aren't married. I also know you've got a daughter in school and it's not easy to pluck her out and take her to a new place. You've got your marine biology work. I've looked into it. It's good work. And the guys who run your project aren't willing to let you out of it anytime soon."

"You talked to my supervisors?"

"Oh yeah. Entitled sons of bitches."

Ryder chuckled, thrilled that Martin and Chuck held their ground with this guy. "You're unbelievable."

"No, I'm just a man who goes for what I want. And I want your girl." He stood, taking his drink with him. "Shall we join the ladies?" he asked, but he walked away from Ryder, leaving his whole body burning with rage.

When he got back to the table, Meade and Jenny were laughing like old friends. He felt paralyzed yet protective of all that was his. "Where is Annabella?" he asked Meade.

"She and Aspen are on the deck. Are you okay? You look a little red."

Ryder ran his hand through his hair, settling himself down as best he could. "I'm fine. I'm just going to go check on Annabella."

He walked outside, passing Annabella and Aspen who barely noticed him. He walked down to the sand, finding a spot below the deck, and leaned against a pole. The thing that frustrated him the most from the whole conversation was that he knew that asshole was right. He needed to let Meade go. It was the only way she was going to do this. It burned him up that Andrew Harrington knew so much about Meade's personality just by looking at her past. Meade had told Ryder her darkest secrets and fears. He earned that knowledge. But as it turned out, anyone who did a background check on her knew her as well as he did.

After he calmed himself, he headed inside and took a seat. The food had come, and all the kids were back at the table. Meade rubbed his back and leaned in. "Everything okay?"

"Yeah. Just got a little nauseous. I'm good." He smiled and kissed her on the lips and then put his attention on his pasta.

Chapter Twenty-Nine

Ryder had been distant all week long. Meade was no dummy. She knew it was something Andrew had said to him when they had gone to the bar and left her with Jenny. When Ryder had come back, he was visibly shaken.

The night had shaken Meade as well. She wasn't expecting Jenny to be so involved in the program. And she certainly wasn't expecting to like her so much.

Ryder had dropped Meade off at her place Sunday night, despite the fact that she had brought an overnight bag with her. But she had not argued, knowing he needed some space and that she needed to give it to him. And she had to admit that she didn't mind having time to process through the night as well. They had texted over the past couple of days, but it was mostly about logistics for the upcoming days she was staying with Annabella.

She sat in the car line at Annabella's school, feeling oddly like a parent. Why couldn't she be? All these other people in these cars were parents. She was as adult as any of them were. Though she was probably a little younger.

Hopefully, at least. She definitely didn't feel old enough to have a fifteen-year-old daughter. She wondered if Ryder felt old enough to have a fifteen-year-old daughter.

The doors opened, and pimple-faced teenagers flooded the area. Annabella walked out with Grace, which didn't surprise Meade. Annabella had told her that they were starting to hang again, and that Grace had changed. Though Meade wished she would not, it was Annabella's life. Meade was not there to judge or talk her in or out of anything.

Annabella spotted Meade, and then said something to Grace. Grace adjusted the straps of her backpack and zoned in on Meade, walking her way. Grace opened the car door, dropping her backpack on the sidewalk, and then got in the front seat. "I know I've been an ass to Annabella. But I'm trying to do better, okay? I like her and I don't wanna lose her as a friend again. That sucked. And I can use a friend right now."

Meade tried to hide her shocked face. "Okay," she said, as if it was neither here nor there to her. But boy, did she love a good redemption story.

Grace got out, and Annabella got in, tossing her book bag in the backseat. "I told you she'd changed. She said that she liked that I didn't back down to her and the guys. And she also said she missed me. She apologized to me. I don't think she apologizes often."

"I imagine that you're right."

"What are we doing right now?"

"I don't know? What do you normally do after school?"

"Go on a shopping spree at the mall?"

Meade smiled, pulling out from behind another car. "How about homework?"

"All done."

"I do have to run by my place to grab my phone."

"Cool," Annabella said, with a little more gusto than

Meade expected.

When they got there, Felicity was lounging in a chair in the backyard, soaking in some sun. "Can you believe this day? Seventy-two perfect degrees."

"Pretty awesome."

Felicity took off her sunglasses and looked Meade up and down. "I thought I was rid of you for the weekend." She winked at Annabella.

"I'm just grabbing my phone. I left it here."

"And you survived the past forty-five minutes? That's a world record for anybody."

Meade went inside and grabbed her phone from where she left it on the bed. Walking back outside, she saw she had several texts from her boss at the bar. "That's not happening."

"What?" Annabella asked.

My boss wants me to come in for a couple hours."

"You can totally do that. I'll stay here and do homework."

"I thought you didn't have any homework."

"I have a little homework. Seriously. Make your boss happy. Go in."

Meade frowned at her, and then she read the text again. "He said it's only till seven." The truth was Meade hadn't been taking as many shifts since she'd been spending a lot of time with Ryder, trying to accommodate his schedule. She could use the money.

"That's perfect. I can finish homework and then we can go have dinner."

"I'll be here," Felicity said.

"Not that I need you to be," Annabella said with a fist on her hip.

"To keep you company. No other reason."

"Are you sure?" Meade asked both of them.

"We are sure," they said in unison.

"Okay, but I'm leaving that bar at seven no matter

what. I'll be back here at twenty after."

Annabella plopped down in the chair next to Felicity. "I'll be here."

Meade wasn't sure why Annabella wanted to stay so badly, but she had her suspicions. "How about I take you home first?"

"Felicity and I are going to hang. Right Felicity?"

"I'm down. Let me see those nails." She took Annabella's hand. "Oh yeah. We've got serious manicures to do. Go."

Meade left the bar half an hour early, which didn't make her boss happy. He had to come out from the back room and watch the bar. But Meade had an uneasy feeling about Annabella wanting her to go to the bar for a while. And she loved Felicity, but Felicity was not a mom either. Annabella wasn't her responsibility.

She opened the door to her apartment, expecting to see one of the twins from next-door there doing God knew what, but instead, she found Annabella with her laptop open. "Homework?"

"Calculus. And I don't even need your help," she said, shutting the laptop. "I am starving though. What are we getting to eat?"

A rush of relief washed over her along with a tinge of guilt. "Anything you want."

As the days wore on, Meade became more comfortable with Annabella. She'd always been comfortable with her, but up until that point, they had functioned more as friends than anything. Now, Meade was starting to feel more like a stepmother.

She'd been preparing healthy meals, checking homework, reminding Annabella of shower time, and waking her up for school. She was relieved when the weekend arrived so they could have some fun.

On Saturday, they shopped and got matching pedicures before Annabella was off to see her friends. Meade took her to Grace's house before dinner, insisting on going in and speaking with Grace's parents to make sure she was comfortable letting Annabella stay. They spoke at length, and Meade left feeling good about the two of them and proud of herself for insisting that she meet them rather than just dropping Annabella at the front door and hoping for the best.

A little after ten o'clock, Meade was doing her final check in with Annabella via text when Felicity strolled into the bar, still wearing her uniform. Desiree had set her up with a job at the catering company she used for events while Felicity interviewed for jobs.

Meade finished her conversation and pocketed her phone. "How was your night?" she asked, pulling out Felicity's favorite cheap, PCB bar wine.

Felicity plopped down on the stool. "You know me. I usually make a good time wherever I am." She winked. "How about you? Have any interesting NASCAR drivers or country music singers come in here tonight?"

"Just a few. I've got them tied to a pole in the back for you when you're ready."

She grinned. "You know me so well." She lost a little of her smile and narrowed her gaze at Meade. "So, have you decided?"

Meade frowned. "Decided what?" Felicity just cocked her head to the side. Meade picked up a rag and wiped down the counter. "I don't have a decision to make."

"Are you sure about that? Because all I heard you talk about earlier this week when you were home was Jenny Harrington. Last I checked you were a straight girl, so I'm thinking you're considering this job."

"I'm not," she said, dunking some dirty mugs into dishwater.

"Have I told you how much I love that you left out that

important little tidbit about the job being with Andrew Harrington when you asked me to help you decide on this job?"

Meade rolled her eyes. "A few dozen times."

"What about Ryder and Annabella coming with you? Is that even on the table?"

"No way. He's a marine biologist. This job is inland. And Annabella is in school. I would never even ask something like that."

"Understood. How's it going with Mr. Perfect anyway?"

Meade checked her phone. "He hasn't been texting me. He's been texting Annabella directly, but I've barely heard from him since he's been gone."

"That's kind of odd."

Meade gave her a look. "Something happened on Monday night. Andrew said something to him. I'm sure of it."

"Ryder's a strong guy. I'm sure he stood up to him."

"Yeah, maybe. But it doesn't mean it didn't get to him. I'm afraid to ask. These days I'm afraid to say much of anything."

"It does sound a bit complicated."

Meade shook her head. "It's always complicated."

Chapter Thirty

Ryder had not slept for days, not even when he was in his own bed earlier in the week. He knew what he had to do, he just didn't know how he was going to do it...or when.

He loved Meade. She'd changed his life. She'd changed him. She made him a better man. She'd given him hope for a happy future for both him and his daughter.

He couldn't begin to think what it was going to do to Annabella when he cut Meade out of their lives. But he had no choice. He couldn't live with himself if he didn't let her go.

He caught an early flight on Saturday. He wasn't supposed to be in until Sunday, but he had to talk to Meade. He didn't know how he was going to execute it, because he was afraid she would talk him out of it. He could see himself being swayed.

When he got home, his house was empty. He called out for both women, but no one responded. He texted his daughter, but nothing. He texted Meade, but she didn't respond either. Were they out somewhere together? He didn't think Meade had a shift that night.

He unpacked, glancing at his phone frequently, but neither female responded. Having enough of the waiting game, he picked up the phone and called Meade. No response.

He needed to be patient. They were somewhere. In this day of technology, if something was wrong, he would be contacted.

Finally, his phone rang and he grabbed it. It was Meade. "Hey," she said, sounding almost surprised. "I saw that you called. Sorry, the bar is loud sometimes."

"You're at work?"

"Yeah. Annabella had a sleepover."

"With who?"

"Grace. She said she told you about it."

He could feel his heartbeat revving up. "She did not tell me about it. You dropped her off over there?"

"Yes. She said she cleared it through you."

"Why didn't you clear it through me?"

"Because you've been barely talking to me this week. I thought you were trying to avoid me."

He pinched the bridge of his nose. "Meade, this is my daughter we're talking about. Why would I be avoiding you when it came to discussing my daughter's care?"

"Everything's fine. I went in and talked to Grace's parents and everything. They were actually really nice."

"I don't care who you talked to. She is not allowed at that girl's house. Not after what happened last time."

"You didn't tell me that."

"I thought it was assumed. You know what she went through over there last time."

"Yeah, I do. But it's different with her and Grace now. Annabella earned her respect."

"Why would you encourage her to be around that girl again?"

"I didn't encourage it. I just dropped her off at a

sleepover that I thought her father approved. Listen, I'm sorry. I'll go get her right now."

"No forget it. I'm home. I'll do it."

"You're seriously going to go pick her up?"

"Yes, I'm gonna go pick her up." He knew he was being over-the-top, but he saw an opportunity and was seizing on it, whether he liked it or not. "I've got to go handle this."

"I'm sorry," she said.

His heart seized at her sincerity. "I'll speak to you later," he said, ending the call. He stood there with his hand on his forehead. He didn't think an opportunity like this would present itself this quickly, if ever. But this was possibly his only way to let her to go so she could do what she really needed to do.

Meade ended the call and stared at her phone like it was a foreign object. Felicity met her gaze with a look on her face that told Meade she had heard everything. "I take it that didn't go well?"

"He completely freaked out. I really think it's fine...her being at Grace's house. I mean, she's not my favorite person, but I saw her with Annabella at school the other day and talked to her for a minute. She's changed. I can tell she respects Annabella now. Annabella and I talked about it and she feels the same way."

"Do you think those boys are going to be over there again?"

"I really don't. I talked with the parents and it sounded like it was going to be dinner and a movie. Like a family night."

"Don't you remember being their age? We always knew how to get out of that kind of stuff. Even at your house."

Meade pursed her lips at Felicity. "You're probably right. I guess I need to go over there and grovel. I'll let him settle down tonight. I'll go tomorrow."

"Probably wise to give it a minute."

Meade shook her head, having a feeling this was not just about Grace.

Chapter Thirty-One

As Meade walked up to Ryder's door, her stomach was tied into every knot a Boy Scout could tie. Ryder had picked a fight with her last night. She knew what she was walking into. She considered letting a handful of days go by in hopes that he would settle down or miss her so much that he wouldn't do this to her. But she knew what she was up against.

When she opened the door, she could see it all over his face. "You're breaking up with me, aren't you?" she said by way of greeting.

He just stared back at her. "You know it's what needs to happen."

Her heart felt like it'd been twisted into a pretzel. "I really don't need a man making my decisions for me. I've made my own decisions for quite some time now and done just fine."

"I'm not making a decision for you. I'm letting you go so I won't be the one who you blame for missing out on the opportunity of working on a space program."

She looked past him, seeing her overnight bag in the foyer. "Wow, you've got me packed up and everything, don't you?"

"I just thought it would be easier this way."

She moved past him, grabbing the bag. She was almost out the door when a wave came over her and she lost control. She turned back to him, pointing at his chest. "I told you I didn't want a relationship. You should've fucking listened to me."

And with that, she was out of his life. .

Chapter Thirty-Two

The nights were the hardest for Meade. Andrew had set her up in an apartment on the compound where many of the staff were housed. The place was sleek and contemporary with expensive artwork on the walls and uncomfortable leather couches in the living room, positioned in front of a television a twenty-something gamer would salivate over. But Meade huddled on the bed most evenings, watching documentaries on her phone. They were out in the middle of nowhere, so there wasn't a library she could hop over to. With her salary, she could download any book she wanted to her phone. But she missed the smell of library books.

And she missed Ryder. And Annabella. They'd become her family. Meade loved her sister, but she'd never been close with her parents. Family was always a struggle for her. But Ryder and Annabella had been easy to love. And she loved both of them.

Annabella texted her once in a while, and Meade always responded, but she never initiated the text. She knew she had to eventually pull away from her, but she wanted to be there for her as long as Annabella wanted her in her life.

She checked Annabella's Instagram. That was a nightly thing for Meade, hoping to get a glimpse into her life or her dad's. Anything to bring her back to Rosemary Beach and that living room couch with the two of them.

But he had let her go. And he had done it for her. That was the hardest part. He made her decision for her, which both pissed her off and made her love him even more.

Andrew's workspace was all open plan. He didn't even have an office. There was a room he went in if he needed to make a phone call, but he liked being on the floor with all the noise and the staff running around.

Meade was stationed next to Jenny. The two of them were practically on top of each other all day, sharing a computer screen often. Sometimes Meade felt like she'd been hired to answer all of Jenny's questions about the universe or to confirm Jenny's suspicions or research on a given subject. Meade wasn't bold enough to ask to be placed on a team that was working on the actual spacecraft. She knew she didn't have her degree in astrophysics or engineering for that matter, and she wasn't about to step into waters where she didn't belong.

But the days were starting to wear on her. What was fun and exciting before was quickly becoming drab and dull. She'd only been there a couple of weeks and knew she had to give it a longer shot than that.

Aspen walked up to their station. "What are you doing?" Jenny asked, checking the desk phone for the time. "You're supposed to be in algebra."

"Mr. Ward isn't here."

"Did Whitney not arrange for a sub?"

"No, because he just didn't show up. She's checking into it. But I'm bored just sitting there." She sat on a clear spot on the desk. "You know, if I had my phone, I wouldn't be bored."

Jenny rolled her eyes at Meade. "I'm never going to be forgiven for taking away their phones before school." She turned to her daughter. "Just look at the chapter you're supposed to be working on."

"You know I don't work well that way. I need to be taught. I don't think that's asking too much."

Meade thought of all the times she'd worked with Annabella on calculus, and her heart pinged. "You said it was algebra?"

"Algebra two," Aspen said, messing with a pen on the desk.

"I can step in," Meade said. "I'm actually pretty good at math."

"Oh God no," Jenny said. "I would never ask you to do something like that."

"No, seriously. I wouldn't mind it at all. I used to help Annabella with math all the time."

"Really?" Jenny asked, and then smiled. "Of course you did. Are you sure you wouldn't mind?"

"Not at all," Meade said, jumping out of her chair. She hadn't been this excited to do something since she got there.

She headed off with Aspen, who took her to the small building next door. There were a handful of rooms, all with state-of-the-art computers, speakers, screens, and wall tablets that looked like something from a sci-fi movie. "I don't know if I can use any of this," Meade said. "Do you have a book?"

"I'll show you how to use it." Aspen walked up to a glass board, and in a moment, what looked like a textbook chapter appeared on the screen. It took Meade a few minutes, but she finally adjusted. "When's your next class?" she asked, realizing she was falling behind on the teaching part.

"I have Mr. Ward for science after this as well. So we're in this classroom until eleven."

"Oh really?" Meade asked, her chest tingling with excitement after the funk she'd been in.

Whitney hustled into the room. "He had a car wreck. He's in the hospital. I feel terrible. I was leaving irritable messages on his voicemail. I've got to go." She gave Meade a curious look. "Do you need something?"

"I'm here to help with math."

"Oh," Whitney said, looking like she was trying to figure out if she was going to allow it or not.

"I'm pretty good at math," Meade said. "I used to help my boyfriend's daughter with her calculus." Just saying the word boyfriend made her heart squeeze.

"Calculus, wow. Annabella's smart," Aspen said.

Whitney narrowed her gaze. "And science?"

Meade just cocked her head to the side.

Whitney closed her eyes and shook her head. "Of course you're good at science. I read your paper and was blown away, by the way." She gave a nervous giggle and then cleared her throat. "I mean, would you mind teaching Aspen's science class after this?"

"No problem at all."

"Thank you."

Meade just smiled with a nod.

Once Whitney was gone, Aspen turned to Meade. "She just went all fangirl on you. Did you see that? I've got to read this paper you wrote sometime. So, you just wrote it and nobody was making you?"

"Pretty much. Or maybe I was making myself."

"Interesting concept. You should stick around here. Maybe you can rub off on me."

"I think you're doing fine on your own, Miss Insta-famous."

She picked at her fingernails. "Yeah, for interviewing celebrities who come to the compound to meet my dad. I wouldn't mind being famous for something like a paper I wrote that nobody asked me to."

Meade was struck by the fact that Aspen wanted more than internet fame. "I'm definitely not famous."

"No, but you're respected. People want you for your brain and not your dad."

The look on Aspen's face broke Meade's heart a little bit. She had no idea a girl so powerful could be so vulnerable. She reminded Meade of Annabella and a blanket of sadness temporarily enfolded her.

"If you hang around me, maybe you'll help me be something other than Insta-famous."

Meade felt terrible for using that terminology. She thought she was giving the girl a compliment, but she realized that maybe young girls needed mentors who could help them gain a love for math and science rather than someone who could help them amass Instagram followers. "How about we tackle today's lessons, then when we're done, I'll show you some super cool stuff that first got me interested in space."

Aspen shrugged. "Okay."

Meade smiled, realizing maybe she was on the verge of finding what could finally settle her lost soul. Teaching.

Chapter Thirty-Three

Ryder had not had it in him to cook for weeks. He'd not been motivated to do the grocery shopping either, and Annabella was tired of cereal and peanut butter. So, they went to Tilly's Tavern for dinner, the restaurant he'd taken Meade to that first night they connected at the library. And as karma would have it, they were seated at the same exact table.

As usual, Annabella was on her phone. He had a no-phone rule at dinner, since it was their time to engage, but he didn't have the energy to tell her to get off it. He just stared at the empty seat where Meade had sat last time they were there.

"I'm jealous. Meade's been teaching Aspen math and science."

Just the mention of her name gave him goosebumps. "What?"

"Aspen's teacher got in some kind of accident, and now he can't teach. So, Meade has taken over his classes."

"She's teaching at a school?"

"Not really at a school. They are at the compound where they all live and work. Apparently, they have teachers on staff. Now Meade is one of them."

"Like for her full-time job?"

"I don't know. Do you want me to ask?" Annabella started thumbing into her phone.

"No. Wait, you still text with her?"

"Yeah. Why wouldn't I?"

He frowned, trying to decide how he felt about that. Honestly, he liked still having a connection to Meade, even if it was through his daughter.

Annabella poked into her phone, and a moment later she said, "Yep. That's her full-time job now. Substitute teacher. And apparently she is going back to school for her teaching degree starting next semester. That's pretty cool."

He sat there with his jaw dropped open. "She's not working for the space program?"

"I don't know. Why don't you just talk to her?"

He didn't know what to say. "But that's the whole reason I let her go...so she could fulfill her dream of working for a space program."

"She only told you about a gazillion times that she didn't want to do that."

"Yeah, but astrophysics is her passion. She wrote that paper. She watches those videos all the time. She reads all those books."

"Did it ever once cross your mind that that is her playtime? I know you love fish and all that, but that's your work. For your playtime, you play that stupid word game on your phone, and you run, and when we were in New Orleans, you used to like to go to those gross flea markets and buy that old furniture and refurbish it. Does that mean you want to own a furniture refurbishment business?"

He thought about it. "No, I don't."

"Maybe she just wants to keep astrophysics to herself.

Maybe she doesn't want to have to do it every day."

He vaguely remembered Meade saying something to that effect, but he'd been too stubborn to listen. He let out a huff of air, realizing what he had done. "I can't believe I let her go."

"I can't believe you did either. It was really stupid, Dad."

"I know." He scratched his head. "Damn."

"You need a much harsher curse word than that."

"I've got to get her back."

"No shit, Sherlock."

He didn't even fuss at her for the language. He just leaned across the table and threw his arms around her, kissing her on the forehead. He sat back in his seat. "Get that phone back out."

"Why?" she asked with a skeptical look on her face.

"Find out what she's doing for Thanksgiving. We're going on a trip."

"Where to?"

"Wherever she's going to be."

Chapter Thirty-Four

Meade typically spent Thanksgiving at her mom and dad's house. But she couldn't take it this year. Maya and Bo were doing Thanksgiving at his parents' house, so Meade would be on her own with her parents. There was no way that was happening. Maya and Bo had invited her to spend it with them, but she couldn't go back to the panhandle. She couldn't take being miles away from Ryder and Annabella on Thanksgiving and not be able to see them.

Which is how she wound up at a catered Thanksgiving dinner with Andrew Harrington's family and a handful of staff members who had hung around for the holiday.

She'd put on makeup and done her hair...even wore a dress because, why not? But what she really wanted to do was go back to her apartment, crawl into the bed, and hope Annabella posted a picture of her and her dad at Thanksgiving dinner.

Aspen had two friends coming, which was the only thing holding up dinner. All day long she'd acted like she had a secret. But after being around Annabella long enough, Meade understood teenage girls were just like that. If Meade had a time machine, she was sure she'd witness herself presenting the same behavior.

Aspen's phone dinged, and she got a huge smile on her face. "They're here! Security is bringing them through now."

Meade looked over at Jenny who was giving her a sad smile. "Are you okay?" Meade asked.

"I'm great. I just really have enjoyed this time with you. I can't tell you how much I appreciate you stepping in with the kids. You've been the best teacher they've had."

"I doubt that since I don't even have my teaching certificate."

Meade had been concerned about that. Apparently, since they were operating under a homeschool situation, a teaching certificate wasn't necessary. But it was for her. It had taken a long time, but she understood now that teaching was what she needed to be doing. It had been under her nose all along, but she had always swept it away, thinking she wasn't good with kids. The truth was, she'd been afraid she was going to screw them up.

But she'd done well with Annabella. She'd built trust with her. Annabella came to her when she needed someone, and Meade was there for her. Annabella was a different girl than she had been a few months ago. She could handle herself now. And Meade liked to think that she had some small part in that.

"Annabella!"

Meade jerked her head around, wondering for a moment if Aspen could read her mind. She had to blink herself awake when she saw Ryder and Annabella walk into the room. Aspen and Annabella embraced, all grins and giggles. Ryder met Meade's gaze with a flushed face as he bit his lip.

Aspen turned to Meade, putting her arm around Annabella. "These are my two friends joining us for dinner."

Meade, glanced around at Andrew and Jenny. By the look on Andrew's face, he was not expecting this company, but the expression on Jenny's face said that she was.

Annabella rushed over and threw her arms around Meade. "I've missed you so much. It's so good to see you."

It was all Meade could do to keep from crying. "I've missed you too. You have no idea."

Annabella squeezed her and then pulled away, leaving Meade and Ryder staring at one another. Ryder walked toward her. "I'm sorry for crashing your Thanksgiving."

"What are you doing here?" Meade asked.

"I was wondering the same thing," Andrew said.

Jenny backhanded him. "I'll explain everything to you. Let's let them talk."

Meade returned her attention to Ryder. "What's going on?"

"Can we talk?"

"Right now? I think they're all waiting for us to have dinner."

Jenny piped up. "We're going to go ahead and get started on Thanksgiving dinner, Meade. When you're done, there will be places at the table for both of you. Feel free to go sit outside by the pool. And take your time."

Ryder raised his eyebrows, and Meade stood there dumbfounded until she could get her bearings. "Okay," she said and led him outside. She was way too antsy to sit, so she just stood there with him by the infinity pool.

"You've quit your job here?" Ryder asked.

"I don't really know what my job here was to be honest. I was more like Jenny's pet. But yes, I've moved into a teaching role."

"And I hear you're going back to school for that?"

She lifted one eyebrow. "Is there anything you don't know about me, Ryder?" she asked, feeling like they were right back in those first few weeks together when she was in flirty mode with him all the time.

He smiled at her just like he did back then with colored cheeks. "I've been keeping tabs, I guess. Is it true?"

"It's a fellowship program for people who have their degrees but just need a teaching certificate. It's a nine-month thing. I'll do it all online so I can continue teaching the kids."

He shook his head at her. "I am so sorry, Meade. I really thought that working here was what you needed."

"I've never known what I needed until now. I don't regret coming here. It really helped shove me into the right thing, even though it's not astrophysics. But I will definitely be teaching these kids astronomy."

He took her hand, and his touch sent butterflies through her belly. "Meade, I love you so much. I only ever let you go because I love you. Do you understand that?"

She nodded, swallowing a lump in her throat.

"I can't take Annabella out of school, but I'll do whatever it takes for us to be together. I'll FaceTime with you for the next two years and nine months or text or have phone sex or anything you want."

"Two years and nine months?" she asked.

"That's when Annabella will head off to college. I can come here then."

She just smiled at this beautiful man she couldn't believe she had landed. "Phone sex for two years and nine months? I don't know if I could make it."

"I'm serious, Meade. You are so different from the person I imagined myself with, but you're so perfect for me. I'm miserable without you. When I think of moving on, it makes me sick. I know I'm not saying any of this the right way, but you're my everything...and you're

Annabella's everything too. We both want you. I'll do whatever it takes. But I've got to keep you in the meantime."

She inhaled a sharp breath, taking in the words she'd been dreaming of him saying. "Last I checked there's not an ocean around here."

"I'll change careers. I'm not kidding. You're the one for me."

She let out a huff of a laugh. "Oh my God. What have I done here? I can't believe I went and let myself fall in love with you."

His eyes went wide and then he closed them. He opened them again and met her gaze. "You love me?"

"Of course I love you, ya big nerd."

He pulled her in for an embrace, and she'd never felt more at home.

She pulled away from him. "I would never ask you to give up your career, just like you would never ask me to give up mine. I've come to love these kids, but I can teach anywhere."

His posture visibly sagged. "Oh, thank God. Because there was no way I could have gone two and a half years without being with you."

"Well, I imagine we would've visited now and then."

He put his hands on her hips. "I can't go two more hours without being with you."

"You might have to. It's Thanksgiving. And we've got dinner waiting for us in there. Our first holiday together, spent with Andrew Harrington and his family. Is this where you thought you'd be having Thanksgiving dinner this year?"

"Not in a million years. But since you've come into my life, there's been a lot of unexpected things."

She nudged a stray hair out of his face. "For me too." It was on the tip of her tongue to say that she never expected to have a stepdaughter, but he wasn't proposing marriage. And she couldn't believe she was even thinking along those lines. "Thanksgiving. We've got to get in there in case they're waiting for us," she said, even though Jenny had said they were not.

"Okay," he said with a grin on his face that let her know she was making the right decision.

They headed into the dining room and got a round of applause as they walked in hand-in-hand. She didn't know these people very well, but she figured most people were suckers for a good romance.

They took their seats next to Annabella. She tossed up her hands. "So, is this happening? Are you coming home?"

Meade had no idea how good it was to hear her use the word *home* in that way. She locked gazes with Jenny. "Not just yet. I've got to finish the school year here with the kids."

"We've already got your replacement lined up," Jenny said.

Meade wasn't sure whether to be relieved or offended. "That quickly?"

"I have a list of subs I call," Whitney said. "I could've called one that day, but I'm glad I didn't."

Meade turned to Ryder and huffed a laugh. "Well, I hope you're ready for me now, because it looks like they're done with me here."

He cupped his hand behind her neck and pulled her in for a kiss that had the whole table whistling. Her cheeks flamed as he pulled away from her, thinking about everyone, including Annabella, witnessing her swooning.

"I'm all in," he said, and she knew for the first time in her adult life that she was on the right track.

The Next Chapter

"To Meade and Ryder, who have more beauty, brains, and bountiful love than any couple should be allowed to have," Ashe said, holding up his cocktail glass.

"Here, here!" came the response from their group.

As Meade and Ryder gazed into one another's eyes with more love and devotion than Felicity had seen in her lifetime, her heart swelled to the point of bursting. She was going to cry right there in Ashe's backyard in front of all of their friends. Partially, her emotions were due to being happy for her friend. But she'd been such an emotional wreck lately that she felt on the verge of tears much of the time.

The year had taken a toll on her. Her whole lifetime had taken a toll on her. She was in such a weird headspace that she couldn't even look for another job. She'd settled for waitressing at a catering company. She hadn't waited tables since college. But it was all she could focus on at the moment.

Sebastian sidled up to her. "Look at our baby, all

married off."

"They're not married yet."

"You know it's just a matter of time."

"True. I don't know if I can handle another bridesmaid dress."

"Do you seriously think Meade would have bridesmaids?"

Felicity chuckled. "I forgot who I was talking about for a minute there."

"How about you? How are you doing, honey?"

She lay her head on Sebastian's shoulder, and he wrapped his arm around her. "I'm doing fine. You can stop worrying about me now."

"You know I worry about all my friends until they're settled into what they need to be doing."

She pulled away. "If you're looking to settle me, it's going to be a while. I have no clue what I need to be doing. Right now, it feels right to be here."

"Then this is where you shall be," he said. "Oh, you know who I saw at the grocery store in WaterColor the other day?"

"Who?" Felicity asked, curious, because everyone they mutually knew in the 30A area was right here at this get together.

"Scott from Maya and Bo's wedding weekend last year."

Felicity's eyebrows went up as her chest tingled. "Oh, what's he doing here?"

Chase and Shayla had chosen that weekend to fall in love, even though Felicity was there as Chase's date, and Scott was there as Shayla's date. And they were all staying together at Chase's house. Awkward didn't begin to cover it.

Felicity and Scott had taken solace in one another. The sex had been amazing, but Felicity didn't know whether he was pounding into her or into Shayla in his mind. He'd tried to contact her when she got back up to Indy, but she'd blown him off. She wasn't anyone's second choice.

"What's he doing in town this time of the year? It's not tourist season."

"He and his extended family are here through the end of this year. He said he lost his mother this year and she was really into Christmas. None of his family could stand to be home during the Christmas season so they've rented a house down here."

"Interesting," she said as she worked out the logistics in her head. How was a whole family mobile enough to drop everything and go on vacation for six weeks?

Sebastian lifted an eyebrow. "How interesting? Didn't you and he…?"

"Yeah, but that's old news."

"Speak of the devil. Isn't that him?"

Felicity's stomach sizzled as she caught sight of Scott hugging Shayla across the yard. Felicity and Scott had only spent one night together, but it had been memorable. It'd been tough for her to ignore his texts, but that's exactly what she had done. However, standing there in her space, he was impossible to ignore.

"Looks like the news cycle could repeat?" Sebastian asked with a grin.

She cut her eyes at Sebastian and then gazed back at Scott. He was only there until Christmas. In the emotional state she was in, she had no business doing anything with a man who she had any potential to fall for.

"Old news needs to stay in the past."

"Got it."

Scott's gaze locked with Felicity's, and she was instantly afraid he was going to make her a liar.

To stay informed of Melissa's new releases, bonus content, and giveaways, sign up for her newsletter at melissachambers.com.

If you enjoyed this story, please consider leaving a review on Amazon. Even a really short review is very much appreciated!

Will Felicity let Scott into her heart on the second try?
Christmas in Santa Rosa coming fall 2022!

Seaside Sweets, Seacrest Sunsets, Seagrove Secrets, WaterColor Wishes, and Grayton Beach Dreams now available on Amazon

Acknowledgments

Thanks as always goes to Kristen Kovach for helping me find plot holes and strengthen my characterization, and for helping me diagnose the occasional medical issue! So proud of you and your huge accomplishment this year!

Thanks to Collin Chambers and Price Kovach for helping me present Annabella as accurately as possible, and for explaining to me the difference between emo, punk, and goth. The devil is in the details!

To the MDA's—how did I ever survive without you! You've turned my publishing and marketing world upside down in the best way! Cheers to all our crazy ideas! Hopefully a few of them will make us proud one day!

To Amy Knupp, my marketing partner and publishing world soulmate. All I can say is it was about damn time that we found each other! I would absolutely not be where I am without your wisdom and guidance this past year. I am not worthy, but I'll take in all the Amy fabulousness that I can get! Keep those texts coming!

And finally, biggest thanks of all to my hubby, Jody, who I'm so thankful for on a daily basis. Love you and that boy more than anything on earth!.

About the Author

Melissa Chambers writes contemporary novels for young, new, and actual adults. A Nashville native, she spends her days working in the music industry and her nights tapping away at her keyboard. While she's slightly obsessed with alt rock, she leaves the guitar playing to her husband and kid. She never misses a chance to play a tennis match, listen to an audiobook, or eat a bowl of ice cream. (Rocky road, please!) She's a member of RWA and has served as the president for the Music City Romance Writers.

Made in United States
North Haven, CT
20 July 2022

21627324R00157